8/22

DISNEY
MULAN

THE STORY OF THE MOVIE IN COMICS

DARK HORSE BOOKS

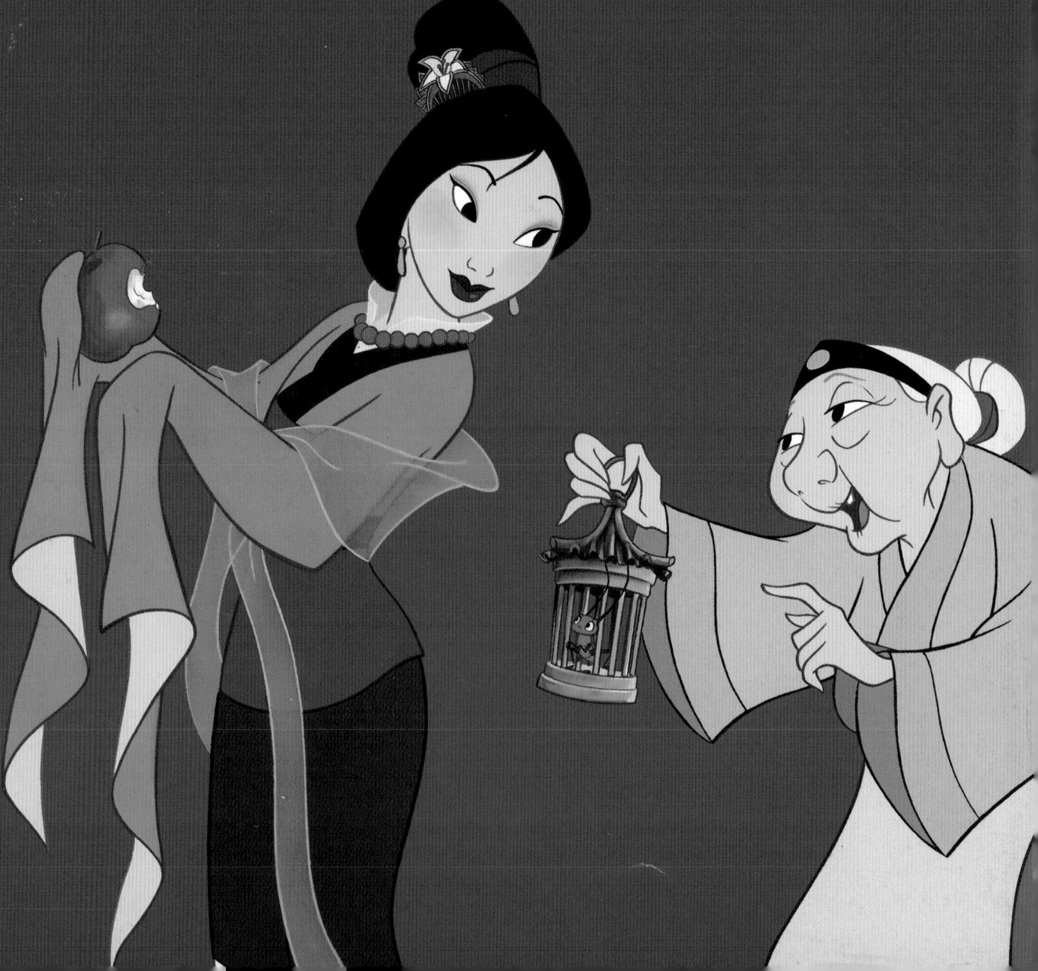

MULAN

MEET THE CHARACTERS

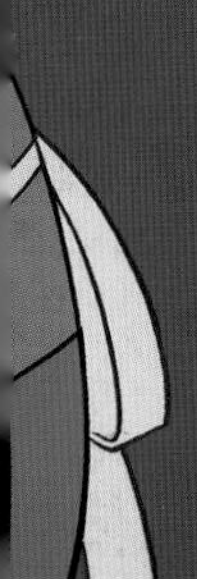

FA MULAN

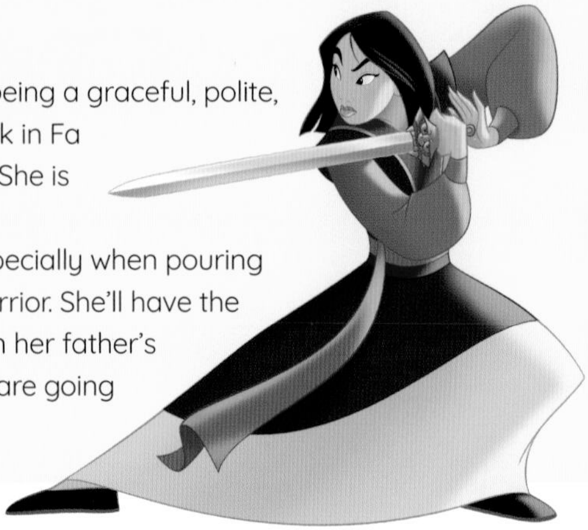

A girl can bring honor to her family only by being a graceful, polite, and obedient wife. This is the way things work in Fa Mulan's world. But Mulan is nothing like that. She is independent, strong-willed, tenacious, and resourceful. She can be clumsy at times—especially when pouring tea is involved—but at heart, she is a true warrior. She'll have the chance to prove it when she joins the army in her father's place, even if she is worried that her actions are going to break her parents' hearts.

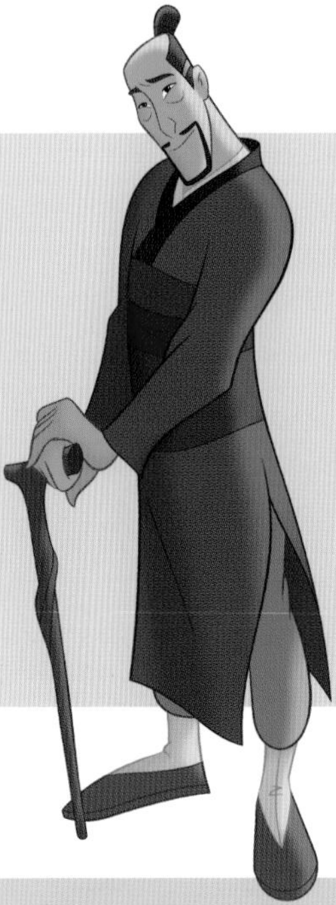

FA ZHOU

A highly respected war veteran, Fa Zhou has grown older and suffered a disabling leg injury: because of this, he is no longer able to fight. But as the only male member of his family, Fa Zhou must serve in the Imperial army when the Huns invade China. Tied to the traditions, he's ready to go, considering it an honor to die for what's right. This is the most important lesson he's ever taught his daughter, Mulan.

GRANDMOTHER FA

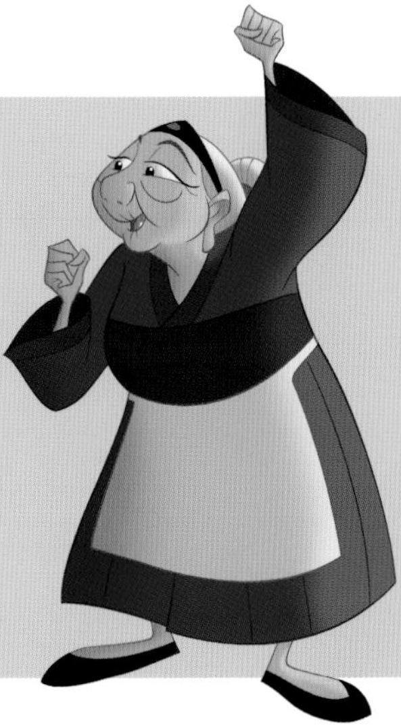

Fa Zhou's mother is witty, spirited, and practical. Well aware of women's role in ancient China, she does her best to help Mulan impress the Matchmaker—the one who evaluates potential wives in the village—but doesn't hesitate to remark on the woman's harsh attitude. Grandmother Fa asks the ancestors to protect Mulan when she disappears to take Fa Zhou's place.

KHAN

Loyal and brave, Khan is the Fa family's horse. Even if he's attached to Mulan, Khan doesn't recognize her when he first sees her wearing Fa Zhou's armor. The horse accompanies Mulan to the army, but he sometimes finds her attempts to act like a man quite funny.

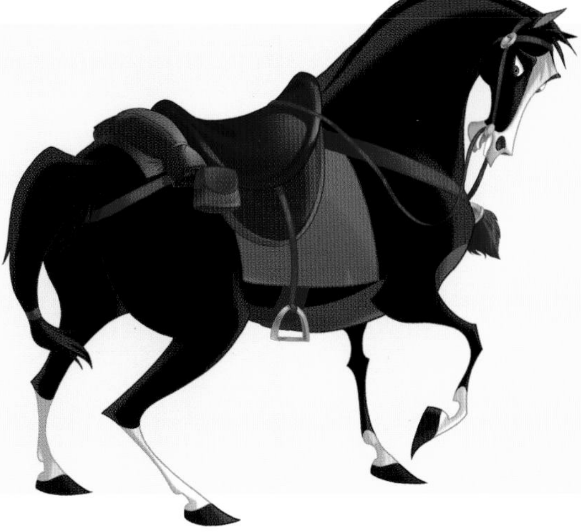

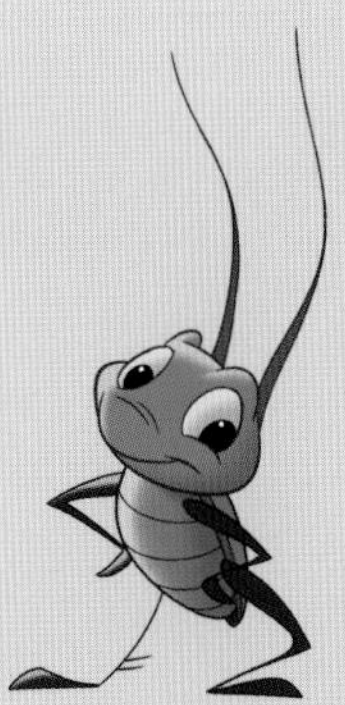

CRI-KEE

Grandmother Fa believes Cri-Kee to be a lucky cricket, and to prove it, she is willing to cross the street with her eyes closed, holding him. She actually survives, but Cri-Kee knows he's not really lucky. Nevertheless, he does his best to help Mulan and Mushu at every opportunity, repeatedly going through great dangers for them.

MUSHU

Demoted from a guardian with the duty of protecting the Fa family to a mere gong-ringer, Mushu definitely has something to prove. Overconfident and impulsive, but with a good heart, Mushu would do anything to regain his former role and be considered a great dragon once again. Turning Mulan into a war hero is how he decides to make it happen.

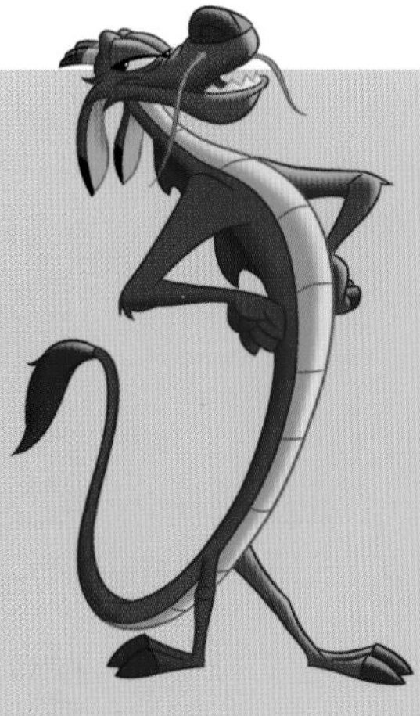

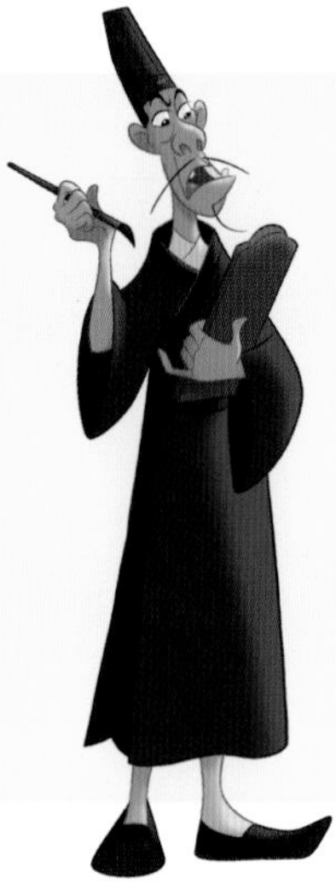

CHI FU

Elitist, arrogant, and strict, Chi Fu considers himself essential to the Chinese empire. As the Emperor's advisor and counsel, Chi Fu executes orders such as delivering conscription notices throughout all the provinces to call up a recruit from each family. Chi Fu despises those who break tradition or the law, and firmly believes women shouldn't talk in a man's presence.

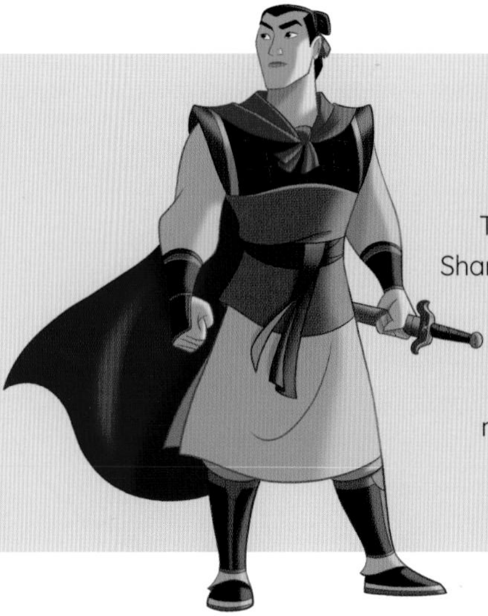

CAPTAIN LI SHANG

The son of General Li, who leads the Imperial army, Li Shang is chosen to train the new recruits. Heroic, fearless, and confident, Shang believes his exhausting preparation will turn them into capable soldiers. Like nearly everyone else, Shang thinks the army is no place for women, but he is prepared to change his mind-set when he realizes how wrong it is.

SHAN-YU

The leader of the Huns is the embodiment of violence. Ruthless and brutal, Shan-Yu believes no army, no man, and no nation can oppose his strength. He's so confident that when he passes the Great Wall, he allows a sentry to light the signal and reveal his presence to all China. Never too far from Shan-Yu is his loyal pet falcon, who is as vicious as his master.

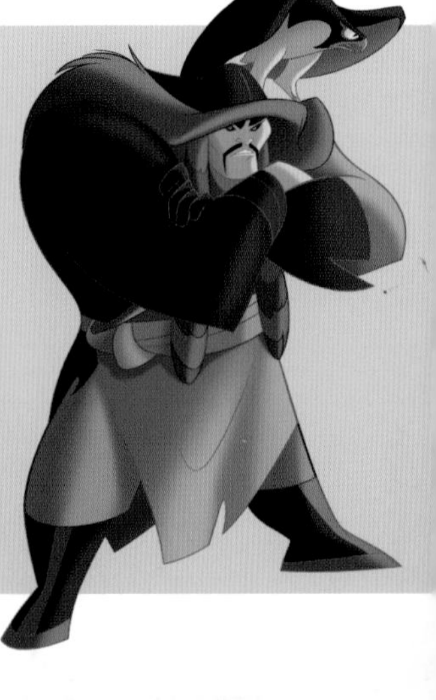

MULAN

THE STORY

"Maybe I didn't go for my father.
Maybe what I really wanted was
to prove that I could do things right."

Mulan

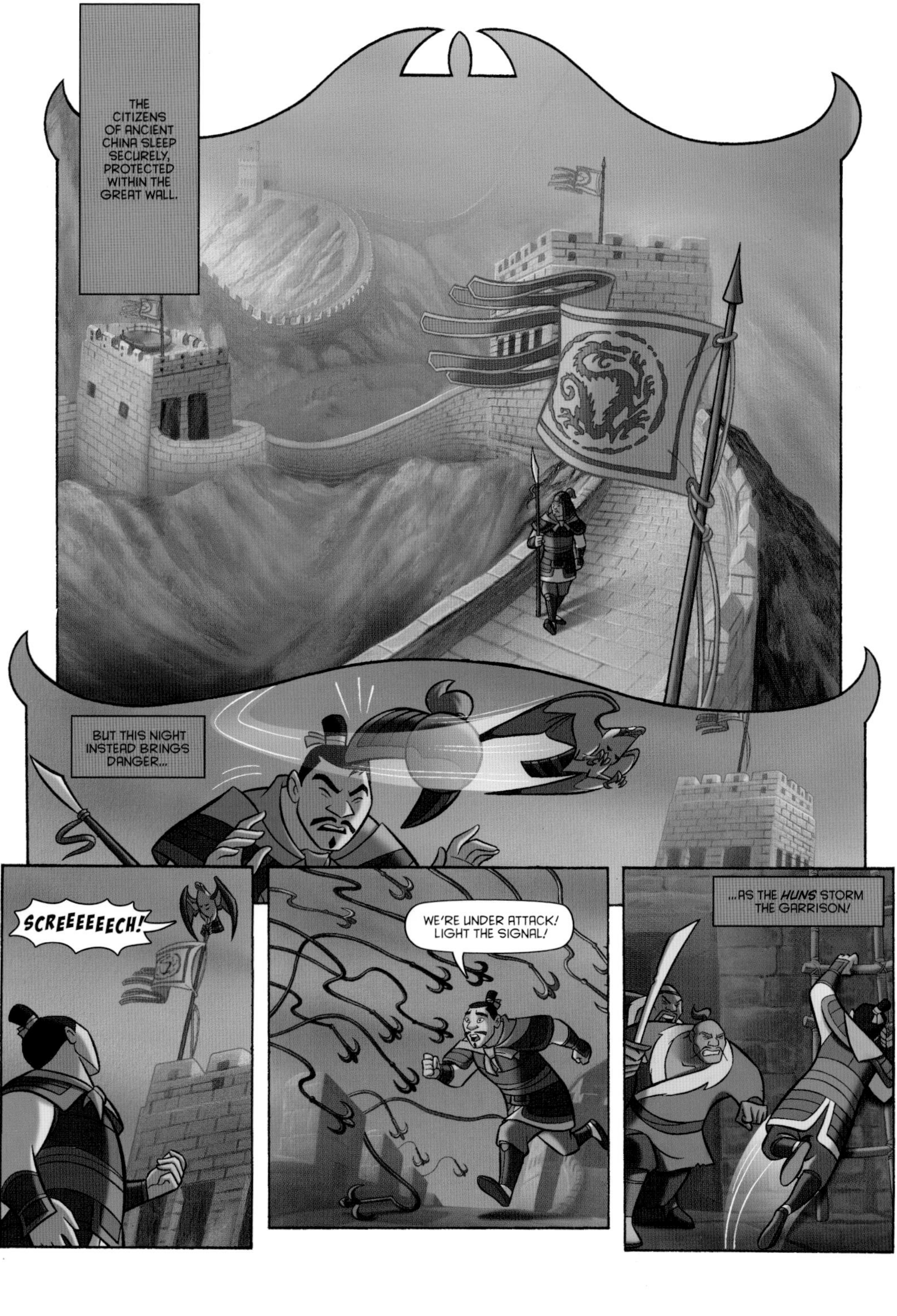
THE CITIZENS OF ANCIENT CHINA SLEEP SECURELY, PROTECTED WITHIN THE GREAT WALL.
BUT THIS NIGHT INSTEAD BRINGS DANGER...
SCREEEEEECH!
WE'RE UNDER ATTACK! LIGHT THE SIGNAL!
...AS THE *HUNS* STORM THE GARRISON!

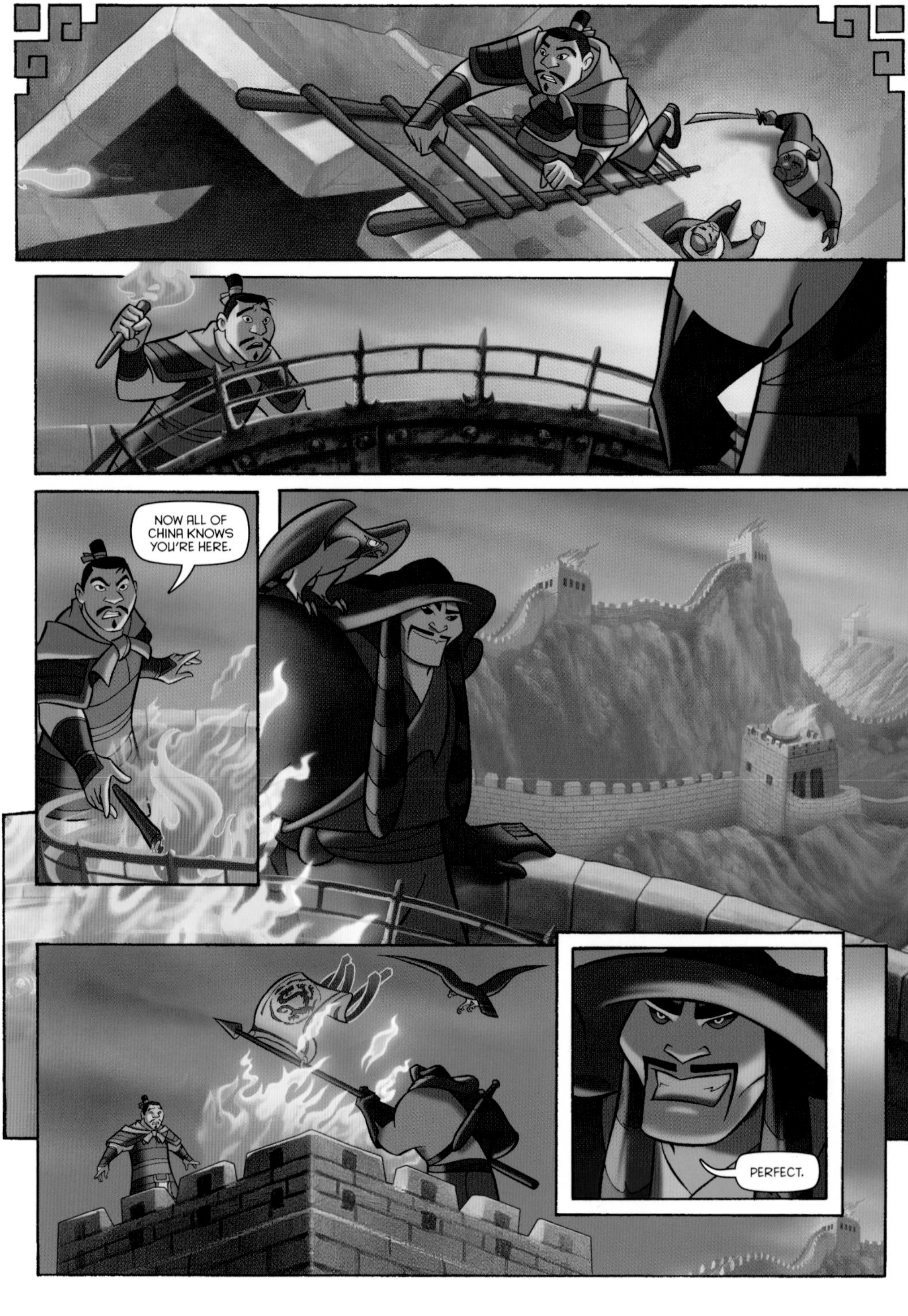
NOW ALL OF CHINA KNOWS YOU'RE HERE.
PERFECT.

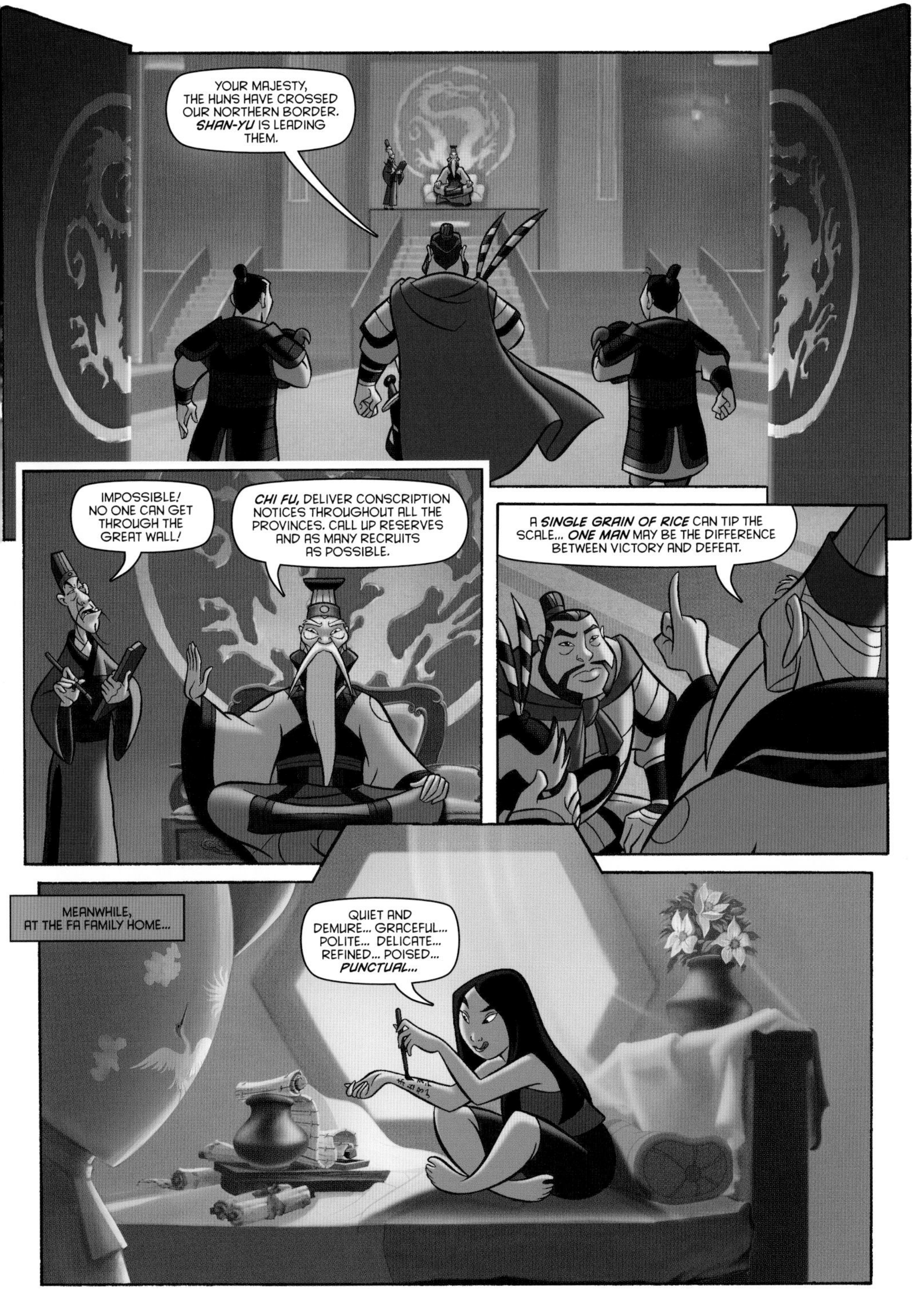
YOUR MAJESTY, THE HUNS HAVE CROSSED OUR NORTHERN BORDER. SHAN-YU IS LEADING THEM.
IMPOSSIBLE! NO ONE CAN GET THROUGH THE GREAT WALL!
CHI FU, DELIVER CONSCRIPTION NOTICES THROUGHOUT ALL THE PROVINCES. CALL UP RESERVES AND AS MANY RECRUITS AS POSSIBLE.
A SINGLE GRAIN OF RICE CAN TIP THE SCALE... ONE MAN MAY BE THE DIFFERENCE BETWEEN VICTORY AND DEFEAT.
MEANWHILE, AT THE FA FAMILY HOME...
QUIET AND DEMURE... GRACEFUL... POLITE... DELICATE... REFINED... POISED... PUNCTUAL...

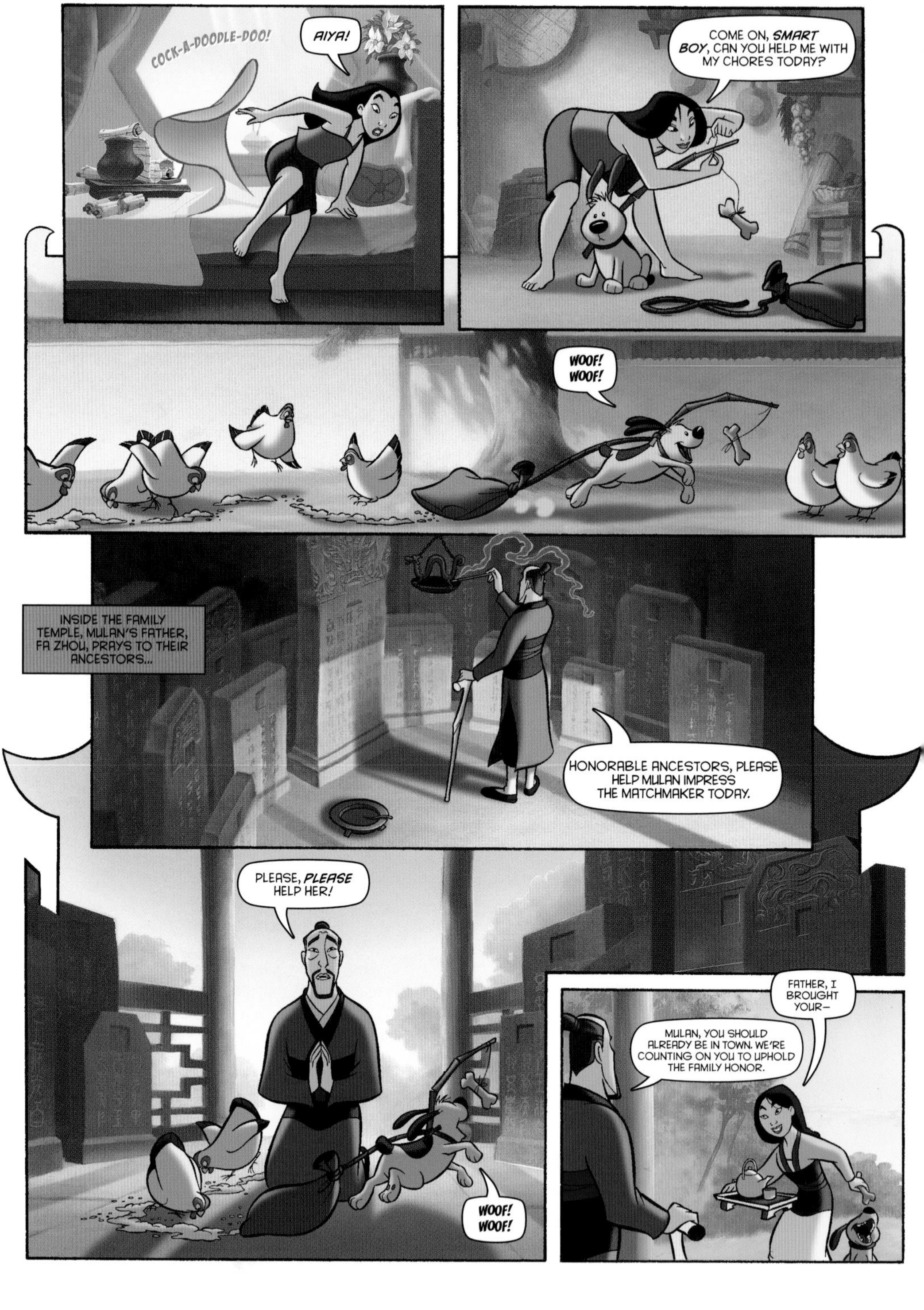
COCK-A-DOODLE-DOO!
AIYA!
COME ON, SMART BOY, CAN YOU HELP ME WITH MY CHORES TODAY?
WOOF! WOOF!
INSIDE THE FAMILY TEMPLE, MULAN'S FATHER, FA ZHOU, PRAYS TO THEIR ANCESTORS...
HONORABLE ANCESTORS, PLEASE HELP MULAN IMPRESS THE MATCHMAKER TODAY.
PLEASE, PLEASE HELP HER!
WOOF! WOOF!
FATHER, I BROUGHT YOUR—
MULAN, YOU SHOULD ALREADY BE IN TOWN. WE'RE COUNTING ON YOU TO UPHOLD THE FAMILY HONOR.

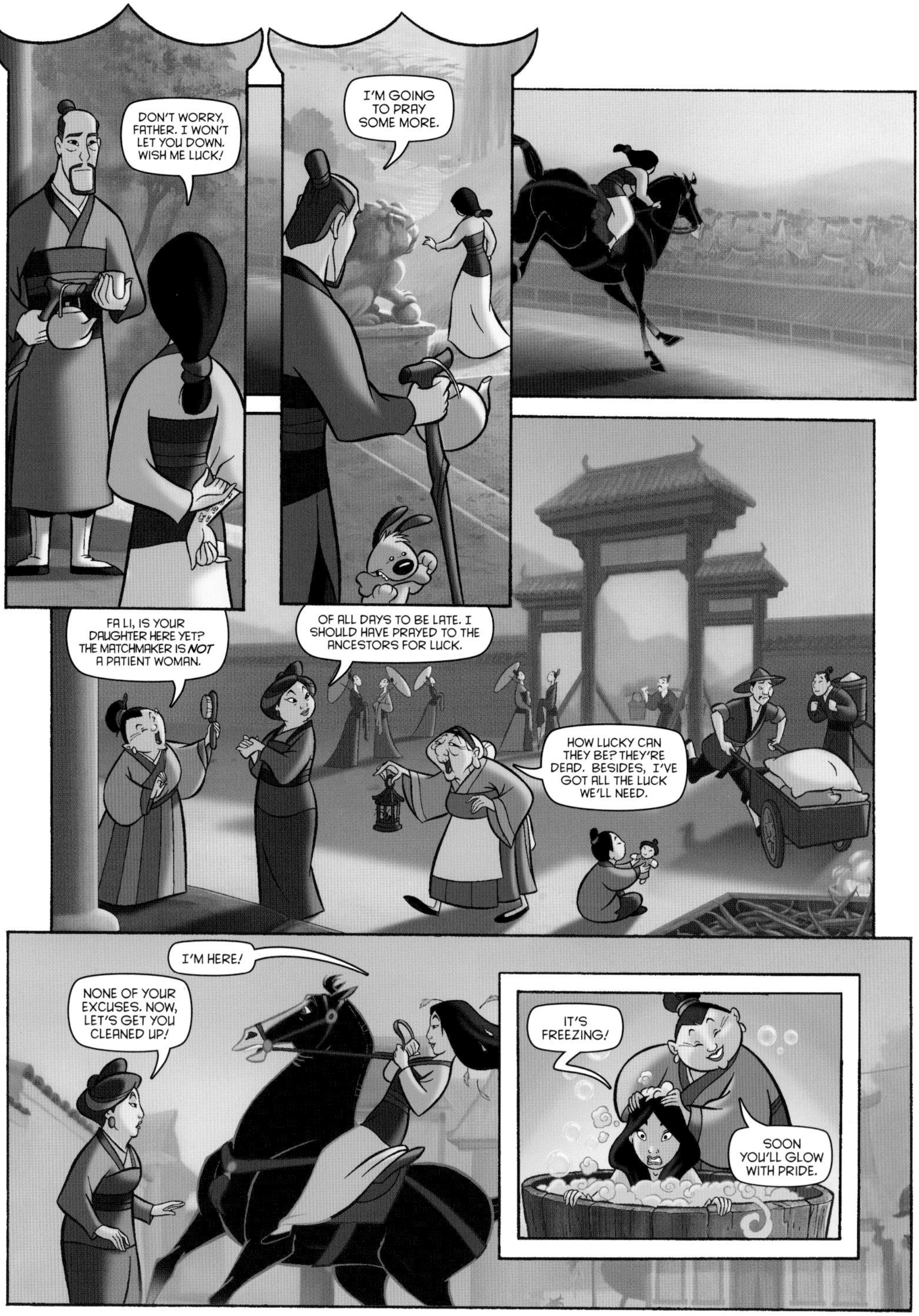
DON'T WORRY, FATHER. I WON'T LET YOU DOWN. WISH ME LUCK!
I'M GOING TO PRAY SOME MORE.
FA LI, IS YOUR DAUGHTER HERE YET? THE MATCHMAKER IS *NOT* A PATIENT WOMAN.
OF ALL DAYS TO BE LATE. I SHOULD HAVE PRAYED TO THE ANCESTORS FOR LUCK.
HOW LUCKY CAN THEY BE? THEY'RE DEAD. BESIDES, I'VE GOT ALL THE LUCK WE'LL NEED.
I'M HERE!
NONE OF YOUR EXCUSES. NOW, LET'S GET YOU CLEANED UP!
IT'S FREEZING!
SOON YOU'LL GLOW WITH PRIDE.

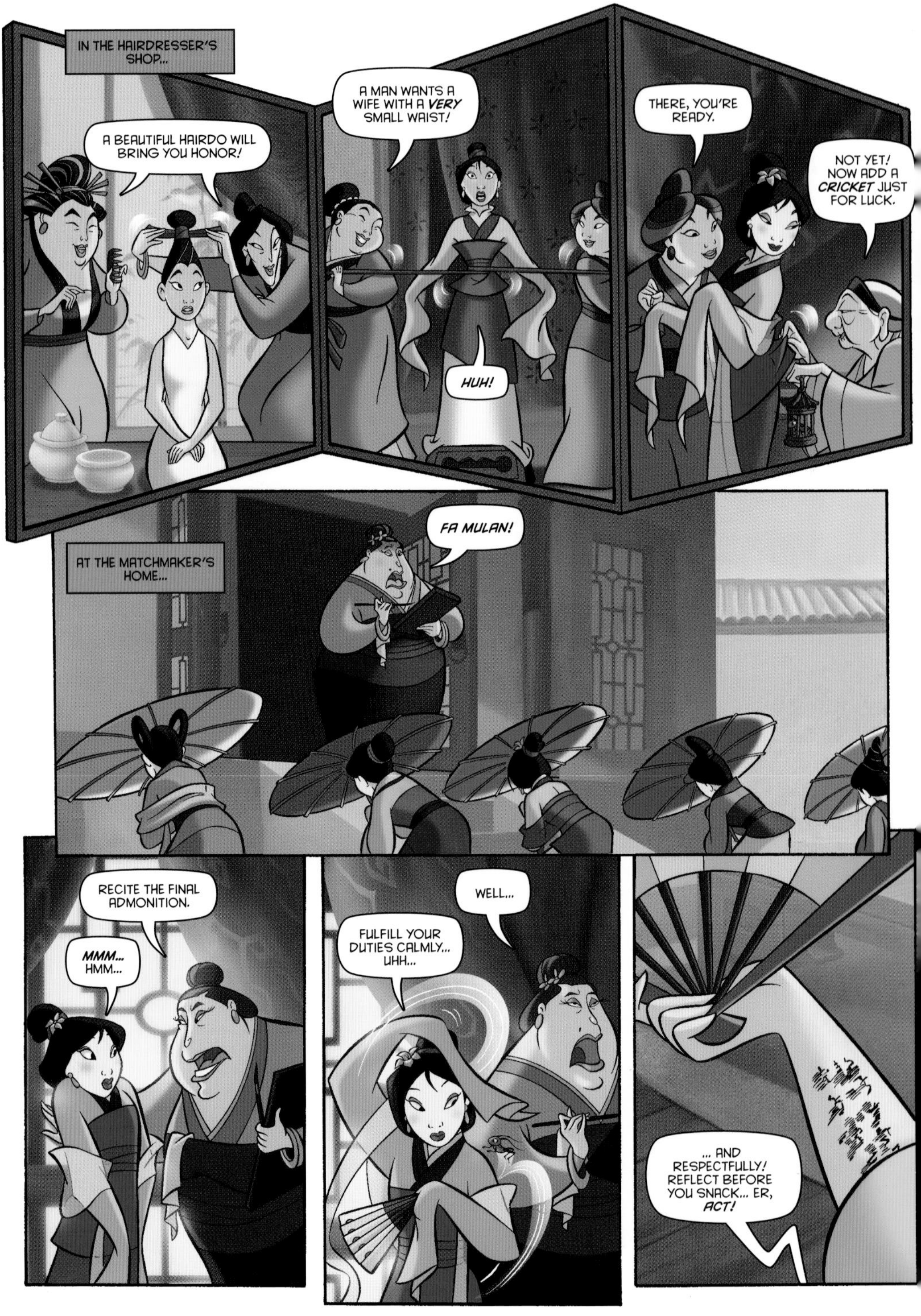
IN THE HAIRDRESSER'S SHOP...
A BEAUTIFUL HAIRDO WILL BRING YOU HONOR!
A MAN WANTS A WIFE WITH A *VERY* SMALL WAIST!
HUH!
THERE, YOU'RE READY.
NOT YET! NOW ADD A *CRICKET* JUST FOR LUCK.
AT THE MATCHMAKER'S HOME...
FA MULAN!
RECITE THE FINAL ADMONITION.
MMM... HMM...
WELL...
FULFILL YOUR DUTIES CALMLY... UHH...
... AND RESPECTFULLY! REFLECT BEFORE YOU SNACK... ER, *ACT!*

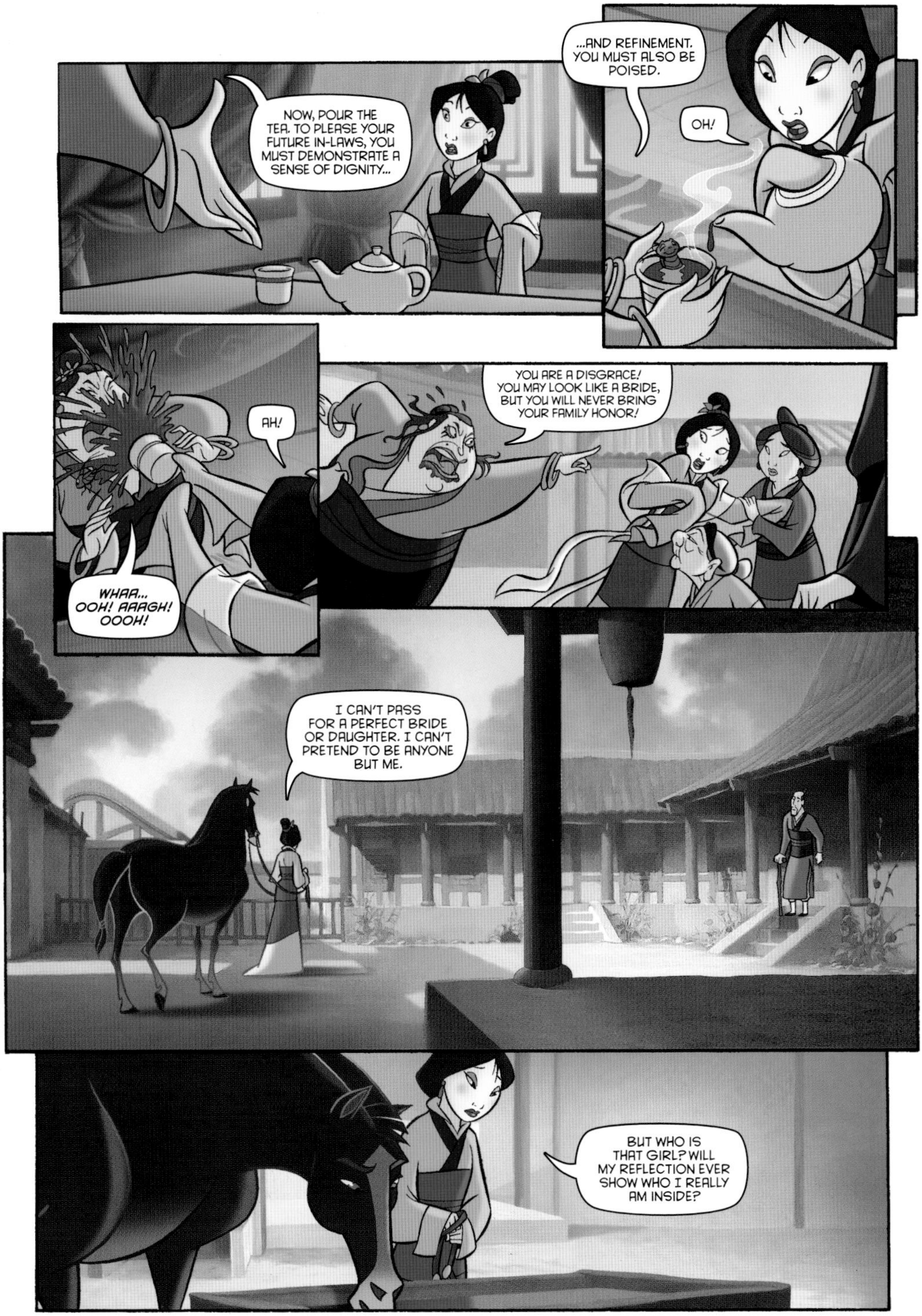
NOW, POUR THE TEA. TO PLEASE YOUR FUTURE IN-LAWS, YOU MUST DEMONSTRATE A SENSE OF DIGNITY...
...AND REFINEMENT. YOU MUST ALSO BE POISED.
OH!
AH!
WHAA... OOH! AAAGH! OOOH!
YOU ARE A DISGRACE! YOU MAY LOOK LIKE A BRIDE, BUT YOU WILL NEVER BRING YOUR FAMILY HONOR!
I CAN'T PASS FOR A PERFECT BRIDE OR DAUGHTER. I CAN'T PRETEND TO BE ANYONE BUT ME.
BUT WHO IS THAT GIRL? WILL MY REFLECTION EVER SHOW WHO I REALLY AM INSIDE?

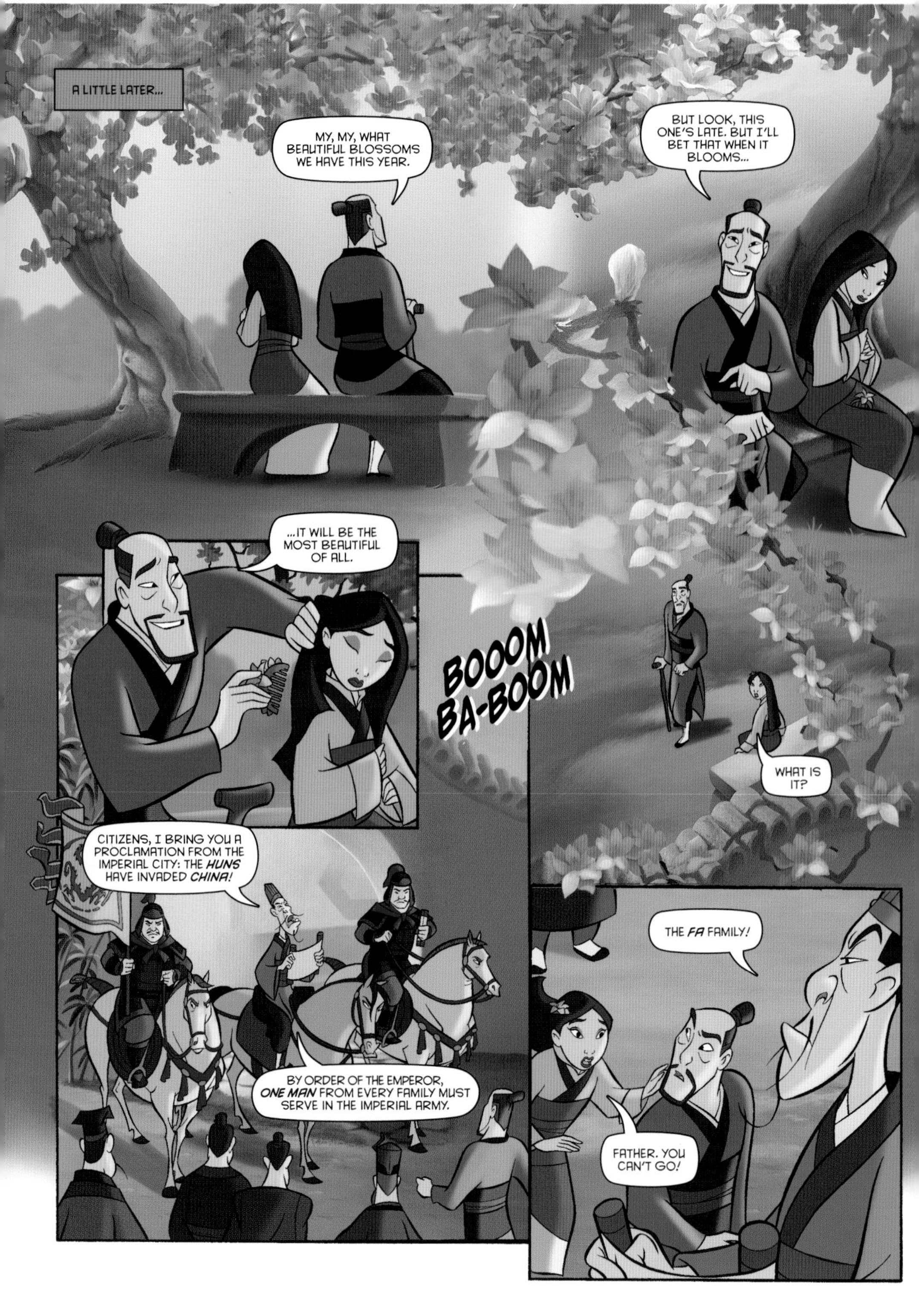
A LITTLE LATER...
MY, MY, WHAT BEAUTIFUL BLOSSOMS WE HAVE THIS YEAR.
BUT LOOK, THIS ONE'S LATE. BUT I'LL BET THAT WHEN IT BLOOMS...
...IT WILL BE THE MOST BEAUTIFUL OF ALL.
BOOOM BA-BOOM
WHAT IS IT?
CITIZENS, I BRING YOU A PROCLAMATION FROM THE IMPERIAL CITY: THE HUNS HAVE INVADED CHINA!
BY ORDER OF THE EMPEROR, ONE MAN FROM EVERY FAMILY MUST SERVE IN THE IMPERIAL ARMY.
THE FA FAMILY!
FATHER. YOU CAN'T GO!

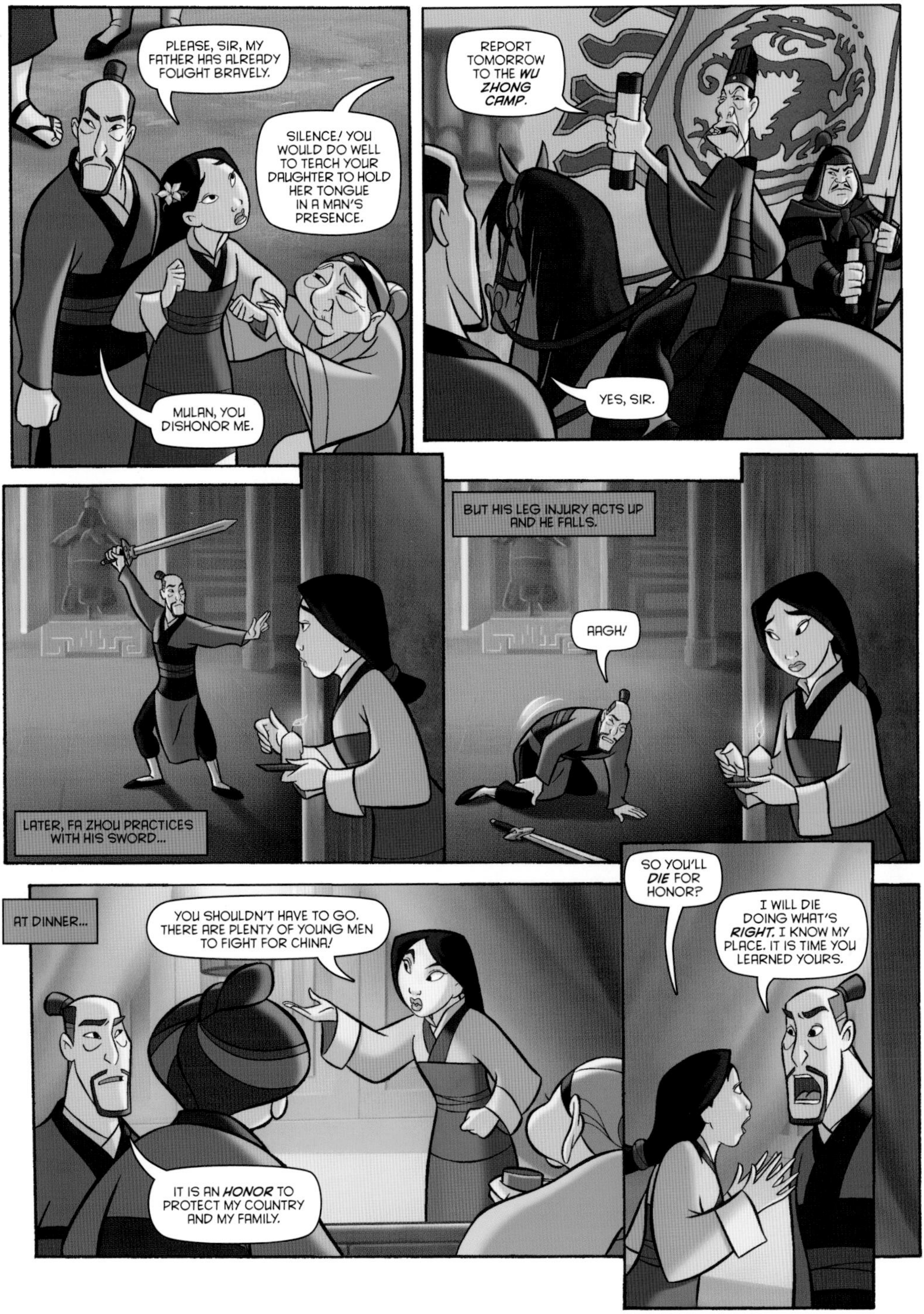

PLEASE, SIR, MY FATHER HAS ALREADY FOUGHT BRAVELY.
SILENCE! YOU WOULD DO WELL TO TEACH YOUR DAUGHTER TO HOLD HER TONGUE IN A MAN'S PRESENCE.
MULAN, YOU DISHONOR ME.
REPORT TOMORROW TO THE *WU ZHONG CAMP*.
YES, SIR.
LATER, FA ZHOU PRACTICES WITH HIS SWORD...
BUT HIS LEG INJURY ACTS UP AND HE FALLS.
AAGH!
AT DINNER...
YOU SHOULDN'T HAVE TO GO. THERE ARE PLENTY OF YOUNG MEN TO FIGHT FOR CHINA!
IT IS AN *HONOR* TO PROTECT MY COUNTRY AND MY FAMILY.
SO YOU'LL *DIE* FOR HONOR?
I WILL DIE DOING WHAT'S *RIGHT*. I KNOW MY PLACE. IT IS TIME YOU LEARNED YOURS.

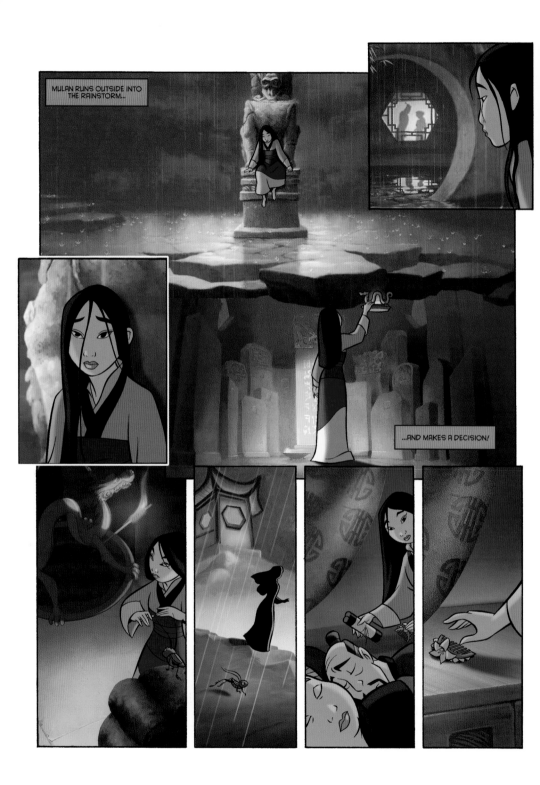

MULAN RUNS OUTSIDE INTO THE RAINSTORM...

...AND MAKES A DECISION!

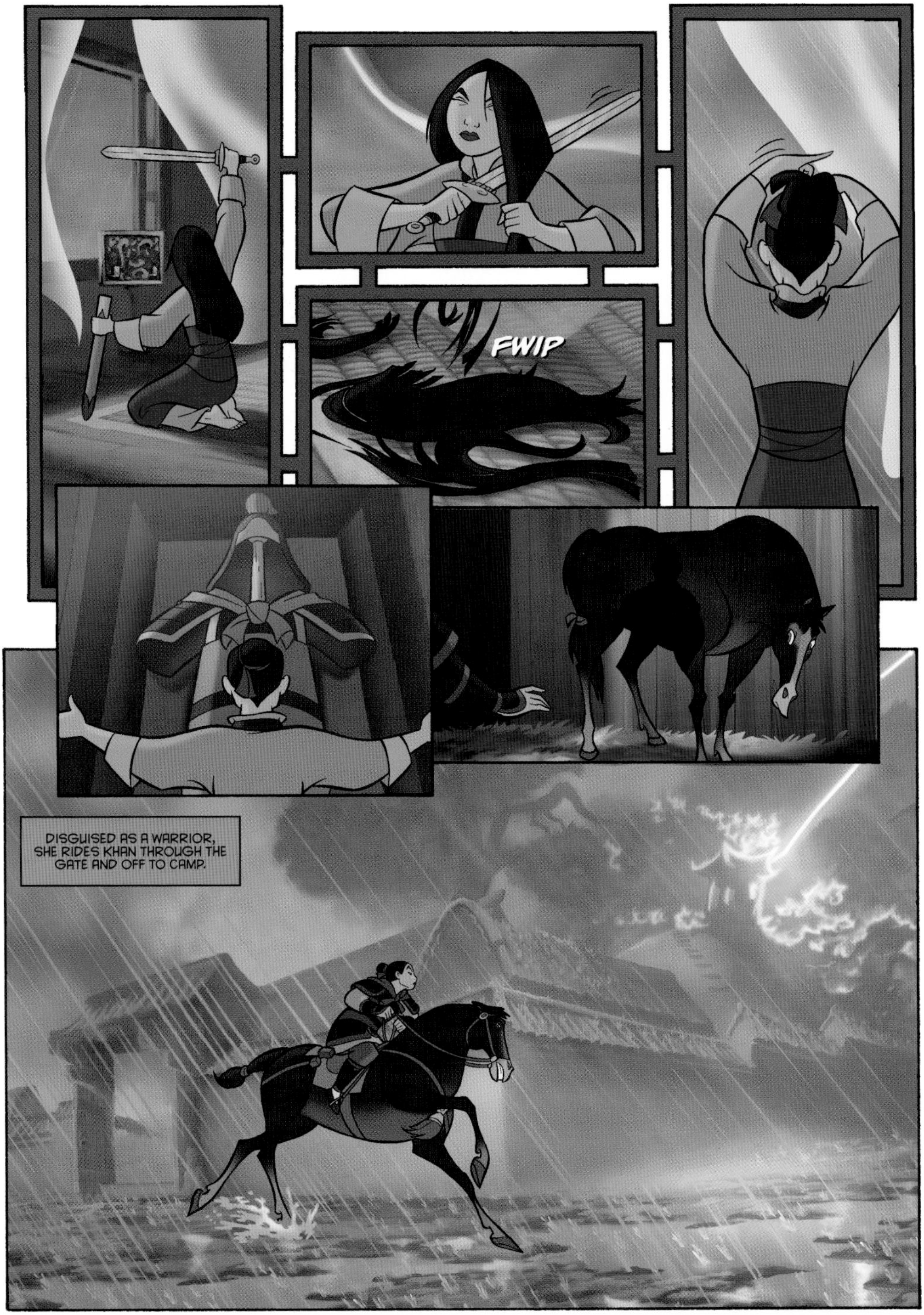
FWIP
DISGUISED AS A WARRIOR, SHE RIDES KHAN THROUGH THE GATE AND OFF TO CAMP.

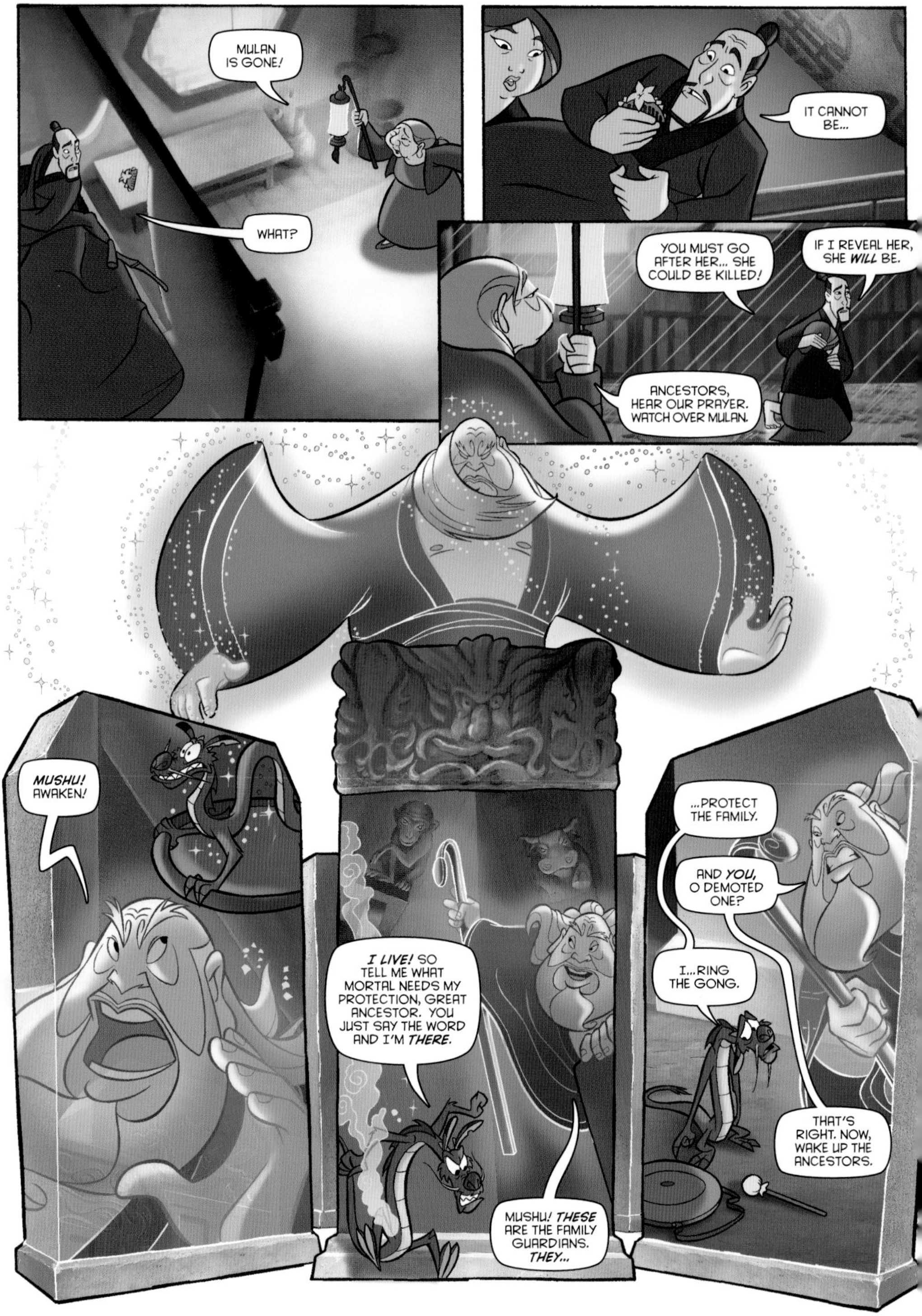
MULAN IS GONE!
WHAT?
IT CANNOT BE...
YOU MUST GO AFTER HER... SHE COULD BE KILLED!
IF I REVEAL HER, SHE WILL BE.
ANCESTORS, HEAR OUR PRAYER. WATCH OVER MULAN.
MUSHU! AWAKEN!
I LIVE! SO TELL ME WHAT MORTAL NEEDS MY PROTECTION, GREAT ANCESTOR. YOU JUST SAY THE WORD AND I'M THERE.
MUSHU! THESE ARE THE FAMILY GUARDIANS. THEY...
...PROTECT THE FAMILY.
AND YOU, O DEMOTED ONE?
I...RING THE GONG.
THAT'S RIGHT. NOW, WAKE UP THE ANCESTORS.

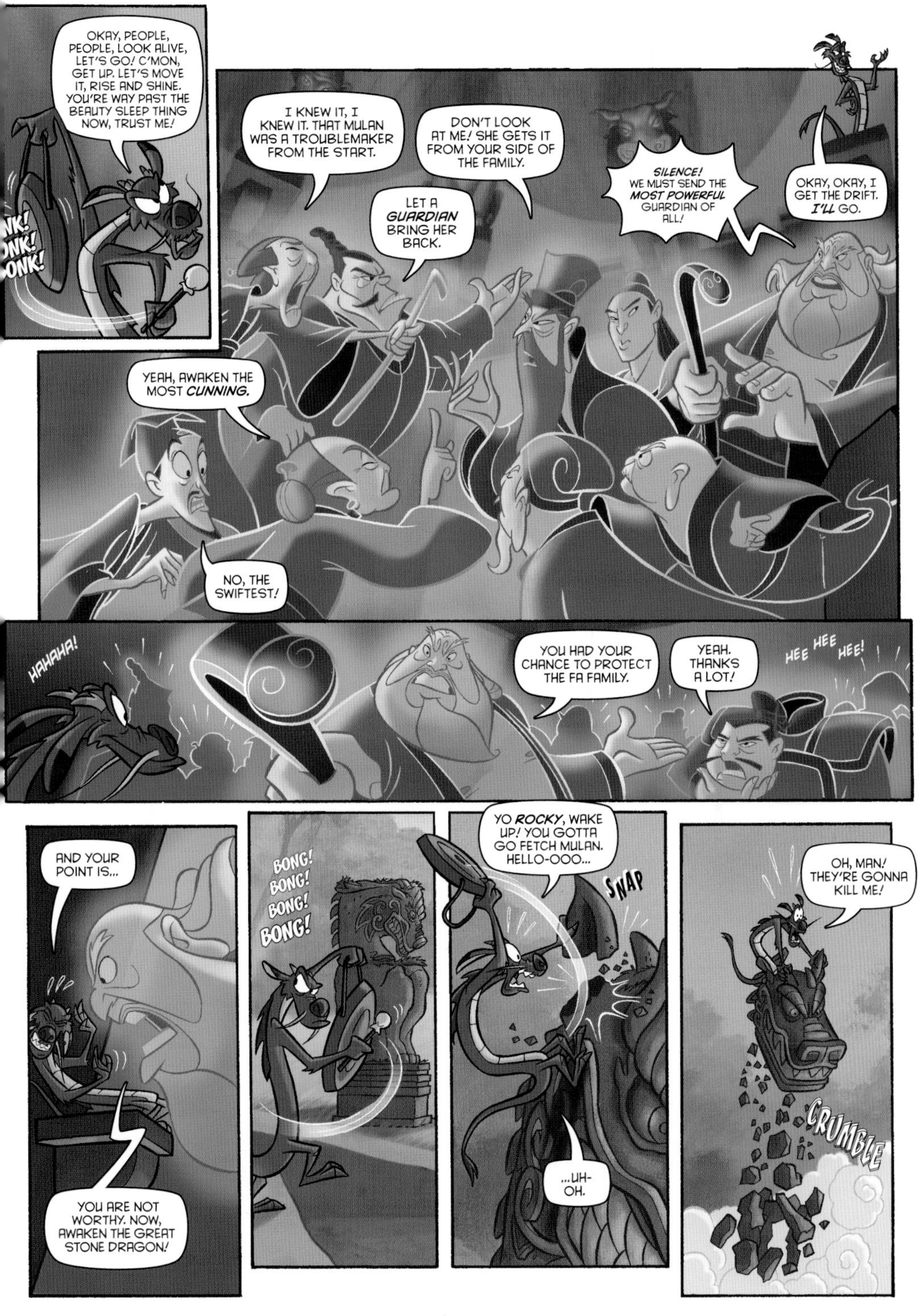
OKAY, PEOPLE, PEOPLE, LOOK ALIVE, LET'S GO! C'MON, GET UP. LET'S MOVE IT, RISE AND SHINE. YOU'RE WAY PAST THE BEAUTY SLEEP THING NOW, TRUST ME!
NK! ONK! ONK!
I KNEW IT, I KNEW IT. THAT MULAN WAS A TROUBLEMAKER FROM THE START.
DON'T LOOK AT ME! SHE GETS IT FROM YOUR SIDE OF THE FAMILY.
LET A **GUARDIAN** BRING HER BACK.
SILENCE! WE MUST SEND THE **MOST POWERFUL** GUARDIAN OF ALL!
OKAY, OKAY, I GET THE DRIFT. ***I'LL*** GO.
YEAH, AWAKEN THE MOST ***CUNNING.***
NO, THE SWIFTEST!
HAHAHA!
YOU HAD YOUR CHANCE TO PROTECT THE FA FAMILY.
YEAH. THANKS A LOT!
HEE HEE HEE!
AND YOUR POINT IS...
YOU ARE NOT WORTHY. NOW, AWAKEN THE GREAT STONE DRAGON!
BONG! BONG! BONG! BONG!
YO ***ROCKY***, WAKE UP! YOU GOTTA GO FETCH MULAN. HELLO-OOO...
SNAP
...UH-OH.
OH, MAN! THEY'RE GONNA KILL ME!
CRUMBLE

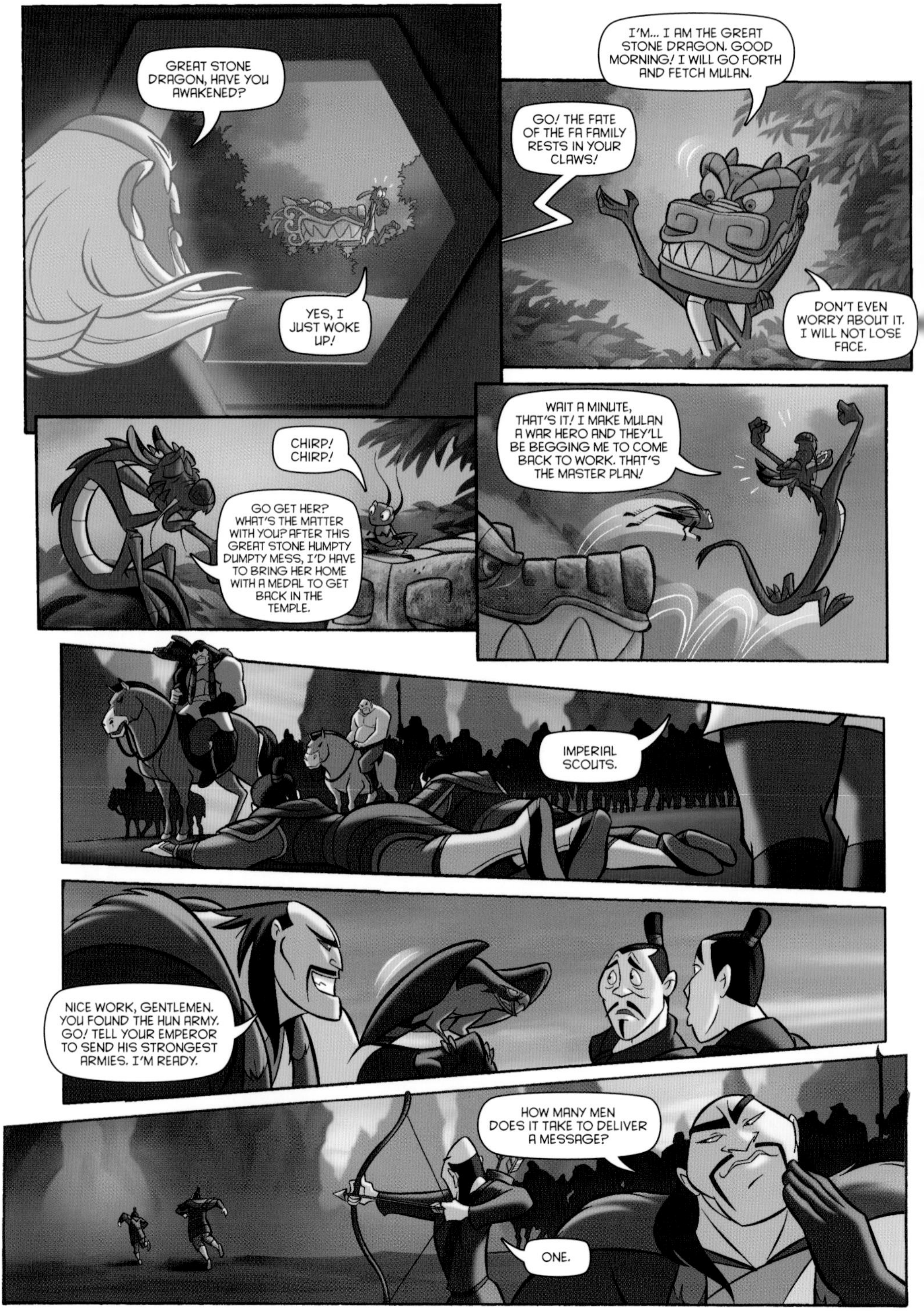
GREAT STONE DRAGON, HAVE YOU AWAKENED?
YES, I JUST WOKE UP!
I'M... I AM THE GREAT STONE DRAGON. GOOD MORNING! I WILL GO FORTH AND FETCH MULAN.
GO! THE FATE OF THE FA FAMILY RESTS IN YOUR CLAWS!
DON'T EVEN WORRY ABOUT IT. I WILL NOT LOSE FACE.
CHIRP! CHIRP!
GO GET HER? WHAT'S THE MATTER WITH YOU? AFTER THIS GREAT STONE HUMPTY DUMPTY MESS, I'D HAVE TO BRING HER HOME WITH A MEDAL TO GET BACK IN THE TEMPLE.
WAIT A MINUTE, THAT'S IT! I MAKE MULAN A WAR HERO AND THEY'LL BE BEGGING ME TO COME BACK TO WORK. THAT'S THE MASTER PLAN!
IMPERIAL SCOUTS.
NICE WORK, GENTLEMEN. YOU FOUND THE HUN ARMY. GO! TELL YOUR EMPEROR TO SEND HIS STRONGEST ARMIES. I'M READY.
HOW MANY MEN DOES IT TAKE TO DELIVER A MESSAGE?
ONE.

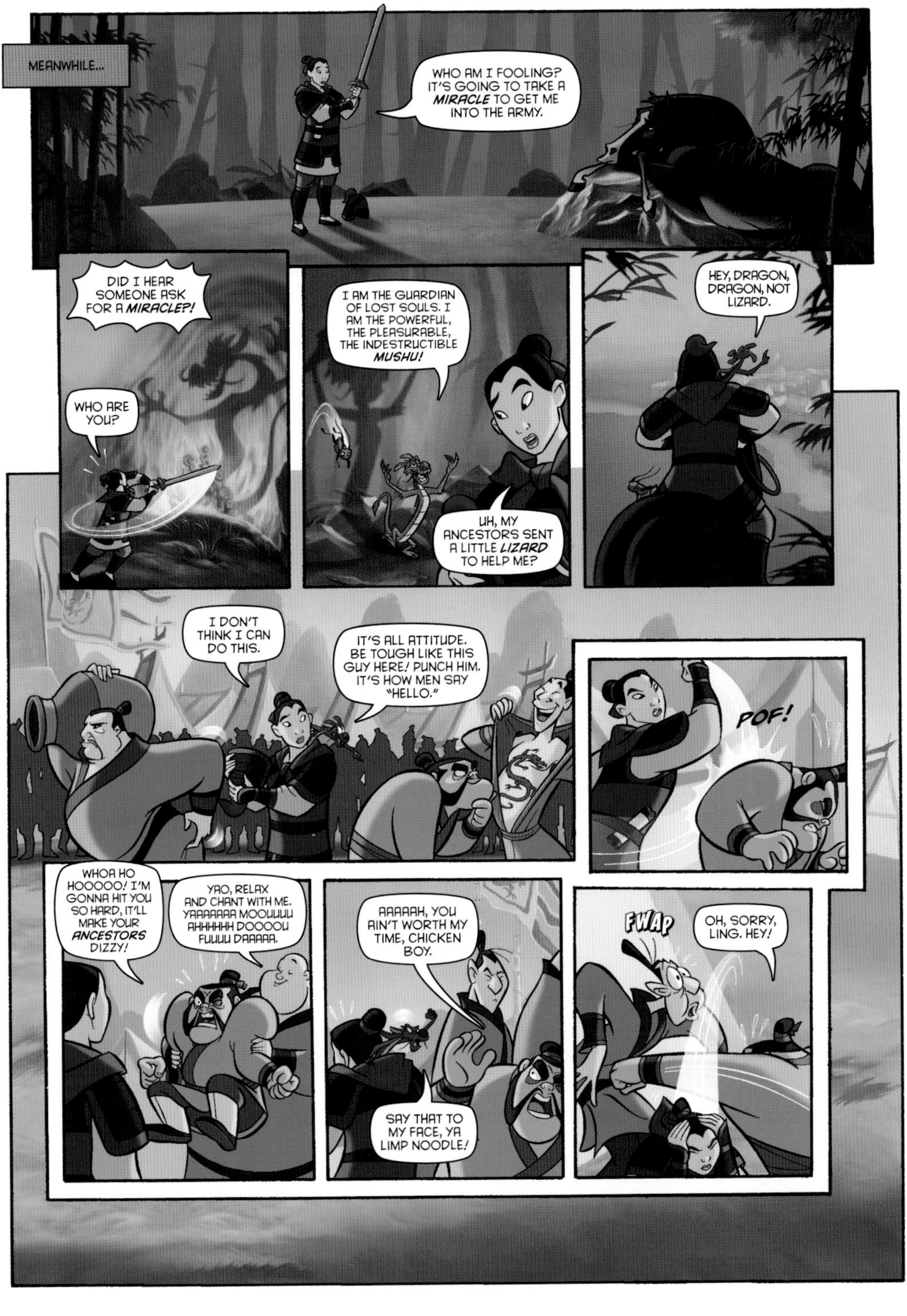
MEANWHILE...
WHO AM I FOOLING? IT'S GOING TO TAKE A MIRACLE TO GET ME INTO THE ARMY.
DID I HEAR SOMEONE ASK FOR A MIRACLE?!
WHO ARE YOU?
I AM THE GUARDIAN OF LOST SOULS. I AM THE POWERFUL, THE PLEASURABLE, THE INDESTRUCTIBLE MUSHU!
UH, MY ANCESTORS SENT A LITTLE LIZARD TO HELP ME?
HEY, DRAGON, DRAGON, NOT LIZARD.
I DON'T THINK I CAN DO THIS.
IT'S ALL ATTITUDE. BE TOUGH LIKE THIS GUY HERE! PUNCH HIM. IT'S HOW MEN SAY "HELLO."
POF!
WHOA HO HOOOOO! I'M GONNA HIT YOU SO HARD, IT'LL MAKE YOUR ANCESTORS DIZZY!
YAO, RELAX AND CHANT WITH ME. YAAAAAAA MOOUUUU AHHHHHH DOOOOU FUUUU DAAAAA.
AAAAAH, YOU AIN'T WORTH MY TIME, CHICKEN BOY.
SAY THAT TO MY FACE, YA LIMP NOODLE!
FWAP
OH, SORRY, LING. HEY!

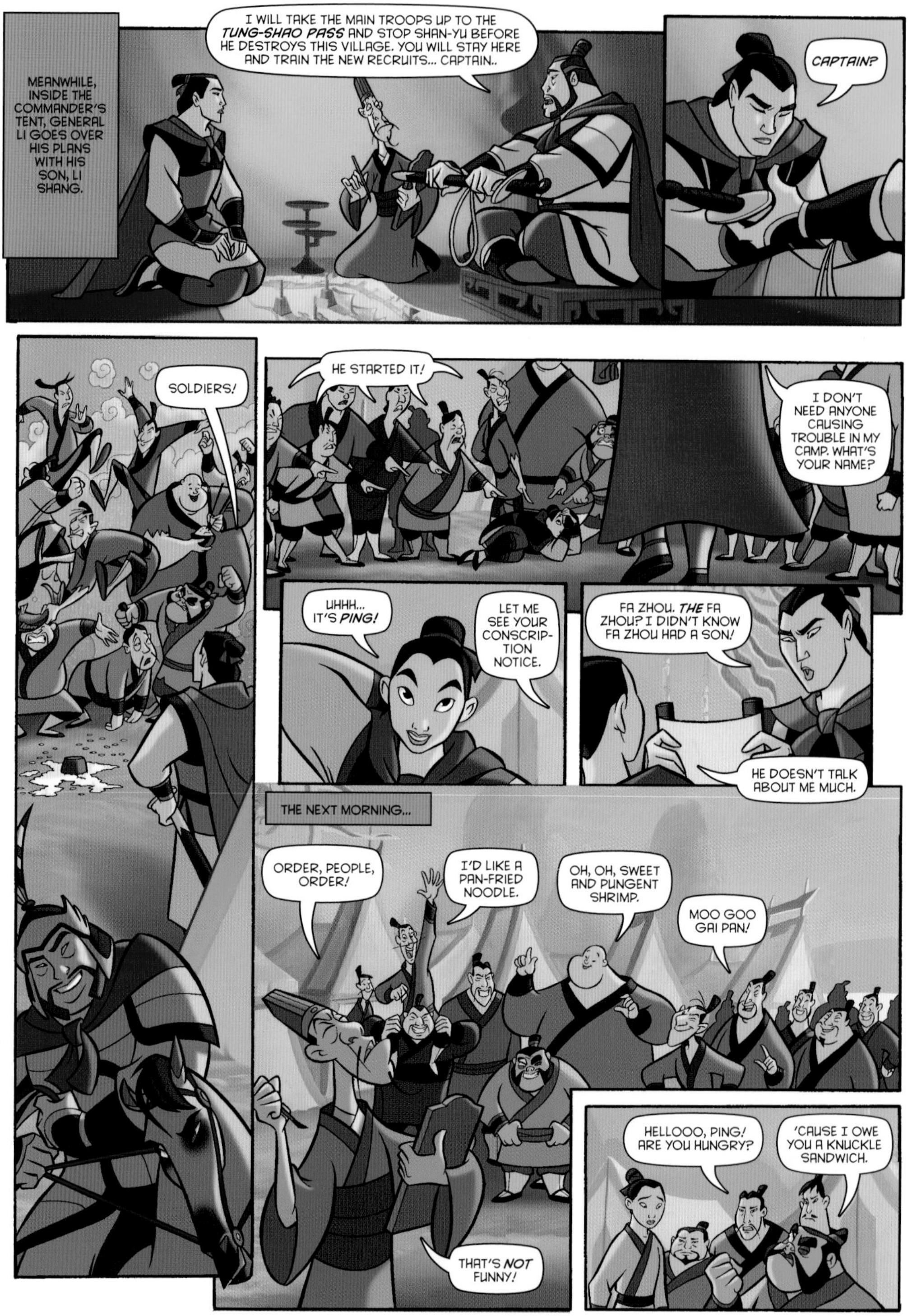
MEANWHILE, INSIDE THE COMMANDER'S TENT, GENERAL LI GOES OVER HIS PLANS WITH HIS SON, LI SHANG.
I WILL TAKE THE MAIN TROOPS UP TO THE TUNG-SHAO PASS AND STOP SHAN-YU BEFORE HE DESTROYS THIS VILLAGE. YOU WILL STAY HERE AND TRAIN THE NEW RECRUITS... CAPTAIN..
CAPTAIN?
SOLDIERS!
HE STARTED IT!
I DON'T NEED ANYONE CAUSING TROUBLE IN MY CAMP. WHAT'S YOUR NAME?
UHHH... IT'S PING!
LET ME SEE YOUR CONSCRIPTION NOTICE.
FA ZHOU. THE FA ZHOU? I DIDN'T KNOW FA ZHOU HAD A SON!
HE DOESN'T TALK ABOUT ME MUCH.
THE NEXT MORNING...
ORDER, PEOPLE, ORDER!
I'D LIKE A PAN-FRIED NOODLE.
OH, OH, SWEET AND PUNGENT SHRIMP.
MOO GOO GAI PAN!
THAT'S NOT FUNNY!
HELLOOO, PING! ARE YOU HUNGRY?
'CAUSE I OWE YOU A KNUCKLE SANDWICH.

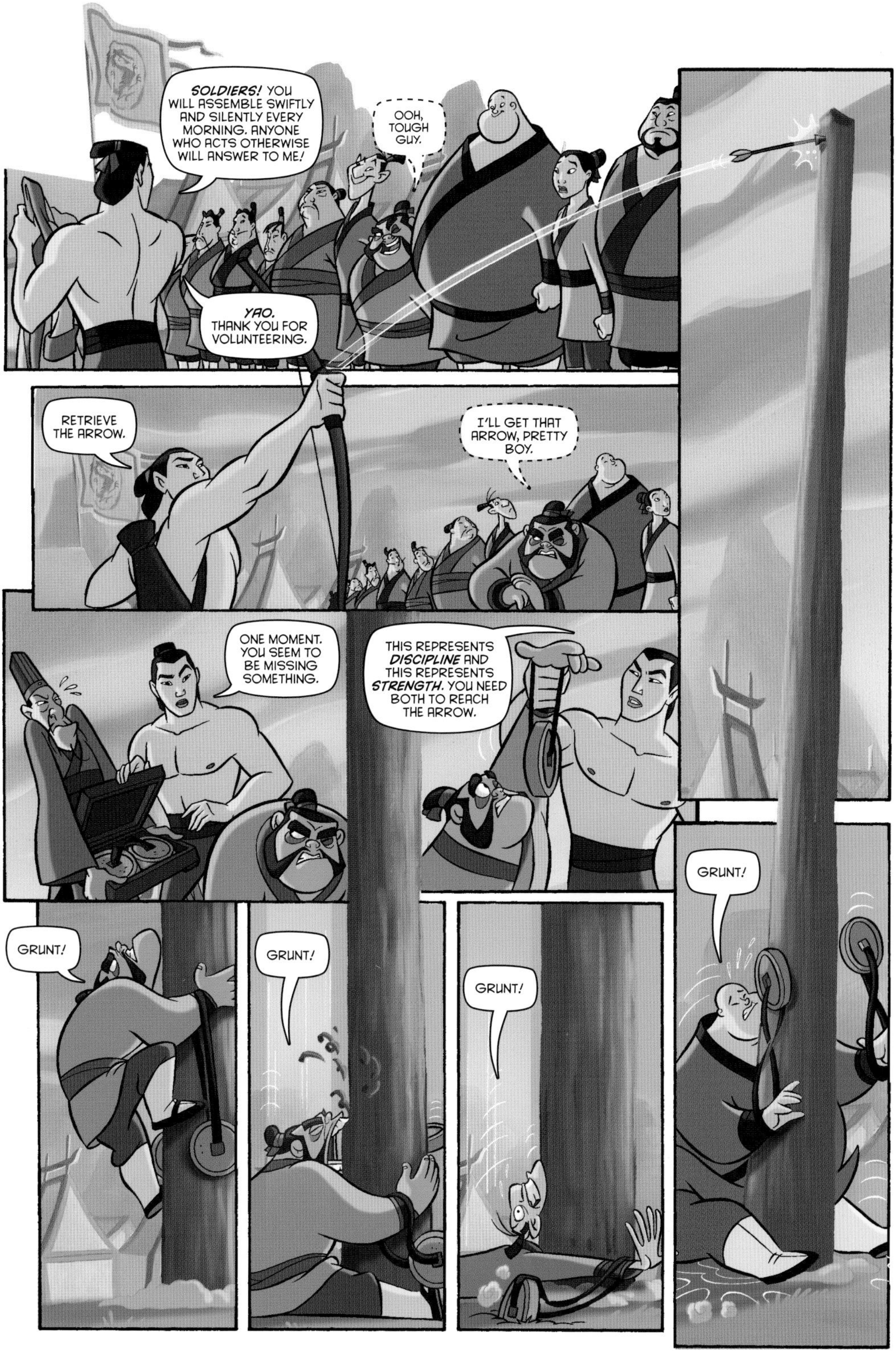
SOLDIERS! YOU WILL ASSEMBLE SWIFTLY AND SILENTLY EVERY MORNING. ANYONE WHO ACTS OTHERWISE WILL ANSWER TO ME!
OOH, TOUGH GUY.
YAO. THANK YOU FOR VOLUNTEERING.
RETRIEVE THE ARROW.
I'LL GET THAT ARROW, PRETTY BOY.
ONE MOMENT. YOU SEEM TO BE MISSING SOMETHING.
THIS REPRESENTS DISCIPLINE AND THIS REPRESENTS STRENGTH. YOU NEED BOTH TO REACH THE ARROW.
GRUNT!
GRUNT!
GRUNT!
GRUNT!

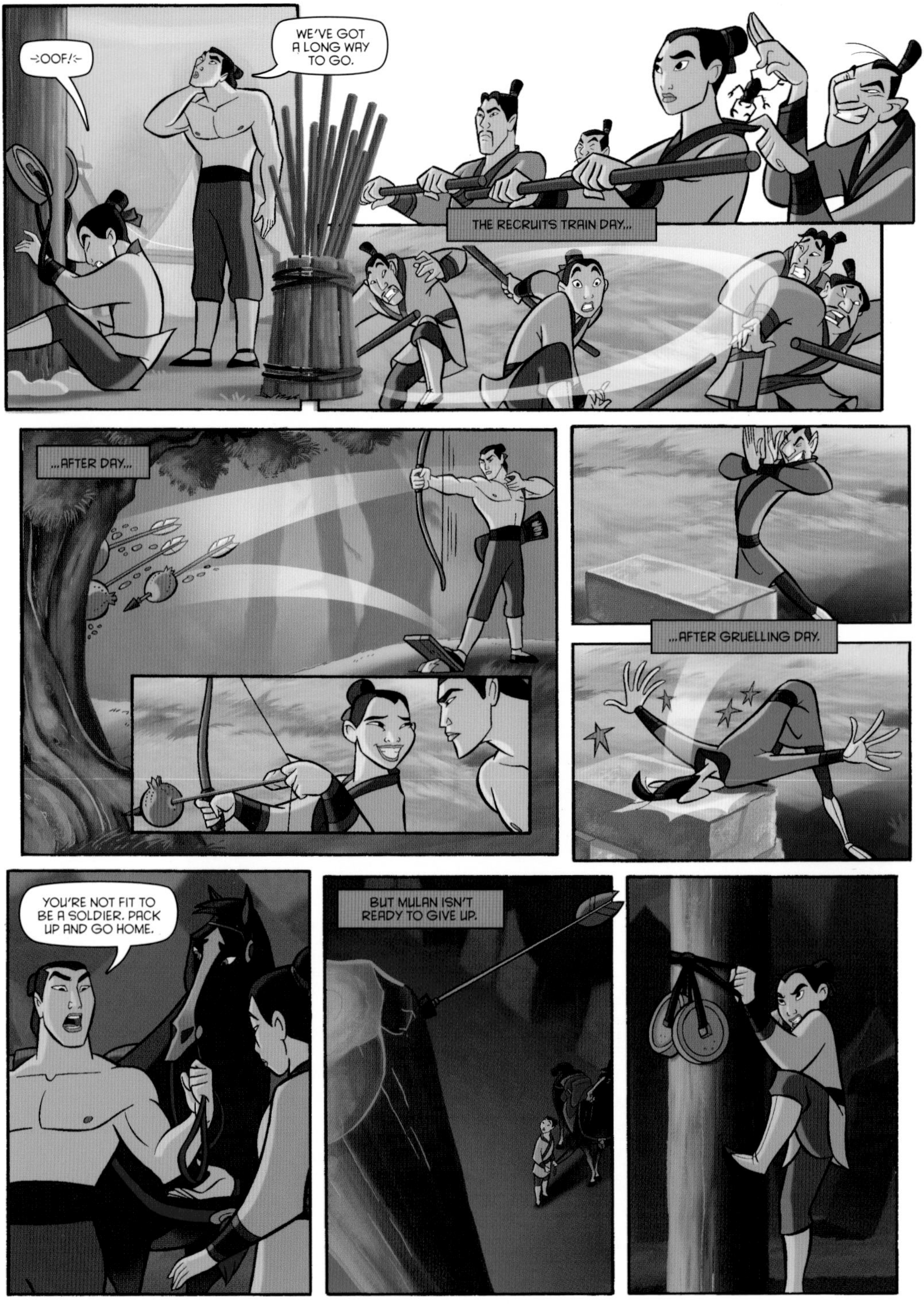
OOF!
WE'VE GOT A LONG WAY TO GO.
THE RECRUITS TRAIN DAY...
...AFTER DAY...
...AFTER GRUELLING DAY.
YOU'RE NOT FIT TO BE A SOLDIER. PACK UP AND GO HOME.
BUT MULAN ISN'T READY TO GIVE UP.

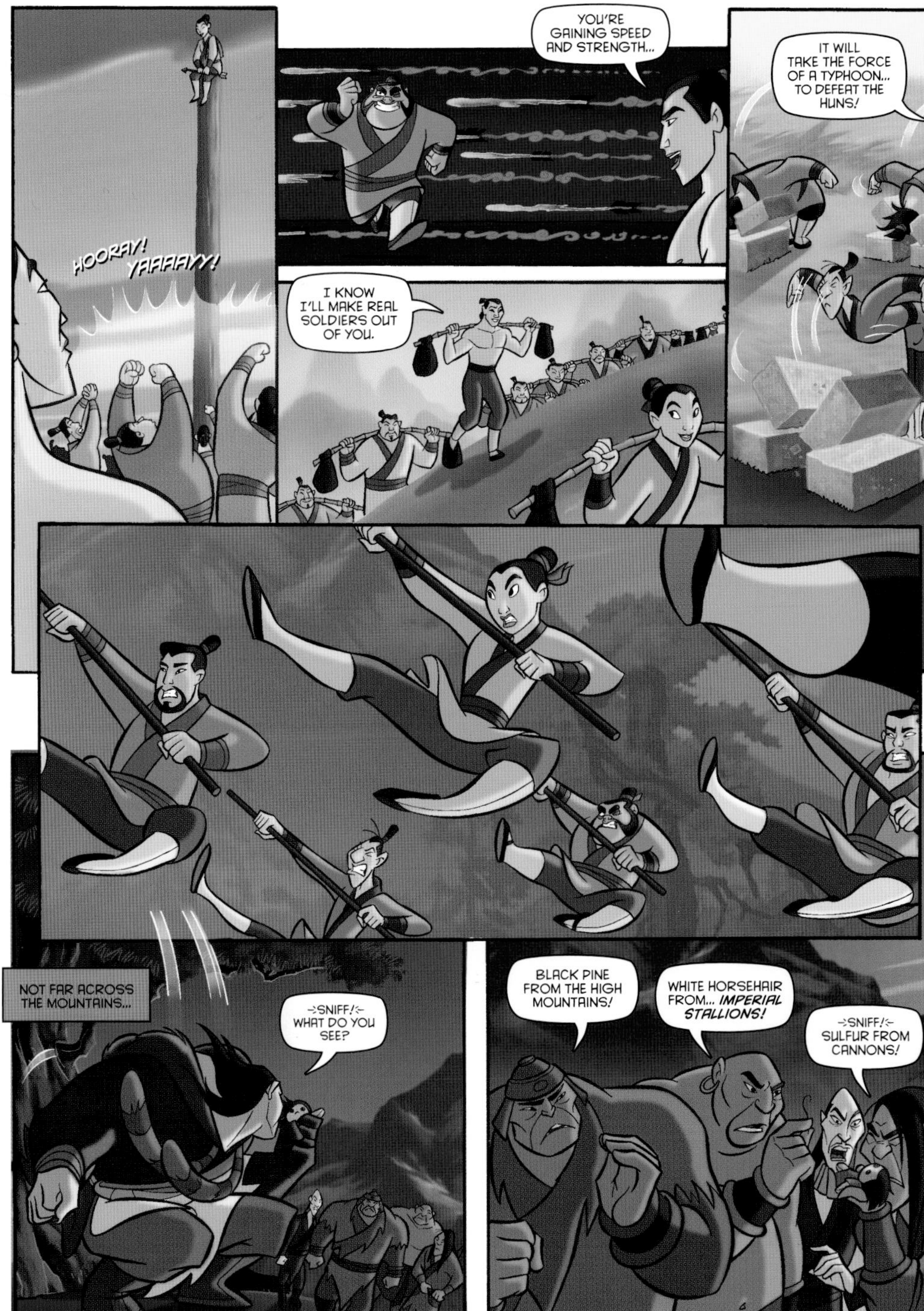
HOORAY! YAAAAYY!
YOU'RE GAINING SPEED AND STRENGTH...
I KNOW I'LL MAKE REAL SOLDIERS OUT OF YOU.
IT WILL TAKE THE FORCE OF A TYPHOON... TO DEFEAT THE HUNS!
NOT FAR ACROSS THE MOUNTAINS...
-SNIFF!- WHAT DO YOU SEE?
BLACK PINE FROM THE HIGH MOUNTAINS!
WHITE HORSEHAIR FROM... IMPERIAL STALLIONS!
-SNIFF!- SULFUR FROM CANNONS!

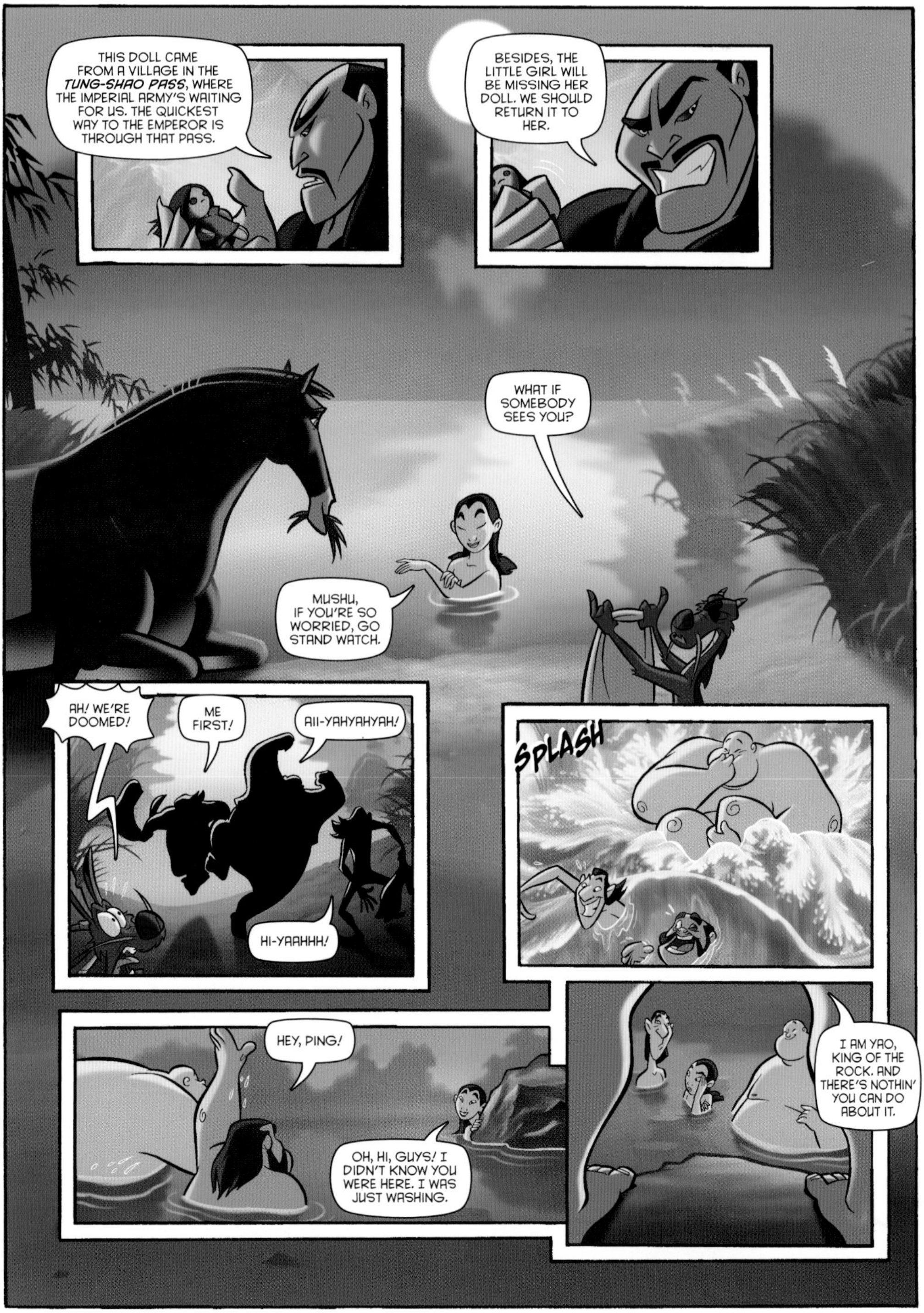
THIS DOLL CAME FROM A VILLAGE IN THE TUNG-SHAO PASS, WHERE THE IMPERIAL ARMY'S WAITING FOR US. THE QUICKEST WAY TO THE EMPEROR IS THROUGH THAT PASS.
BESIDES, THE LITTLE GIRL WILL BE MISSING HER DOLL. WE SHOULD RETURN IT TO HER.
WHAT IF SOMEBODY SEES YOU?
MUSHU, IF YOU'RE SO WORRIED, GO STAND WATCH.
AH! WE'RE DOOMED!
ME FIRST!
AII-YAHYAHYAH!
HI-YAAHHH!
SPLASH
HEY, PING!
OH, HI, GUYS! I DIDN'T KNOW YOU WERE HERE. I WAS JUST WASHING.
I AM YAO, KING OF THE ROCK. AND THERE'S NOTHIN' YOU CAN DO ABOUT IT.

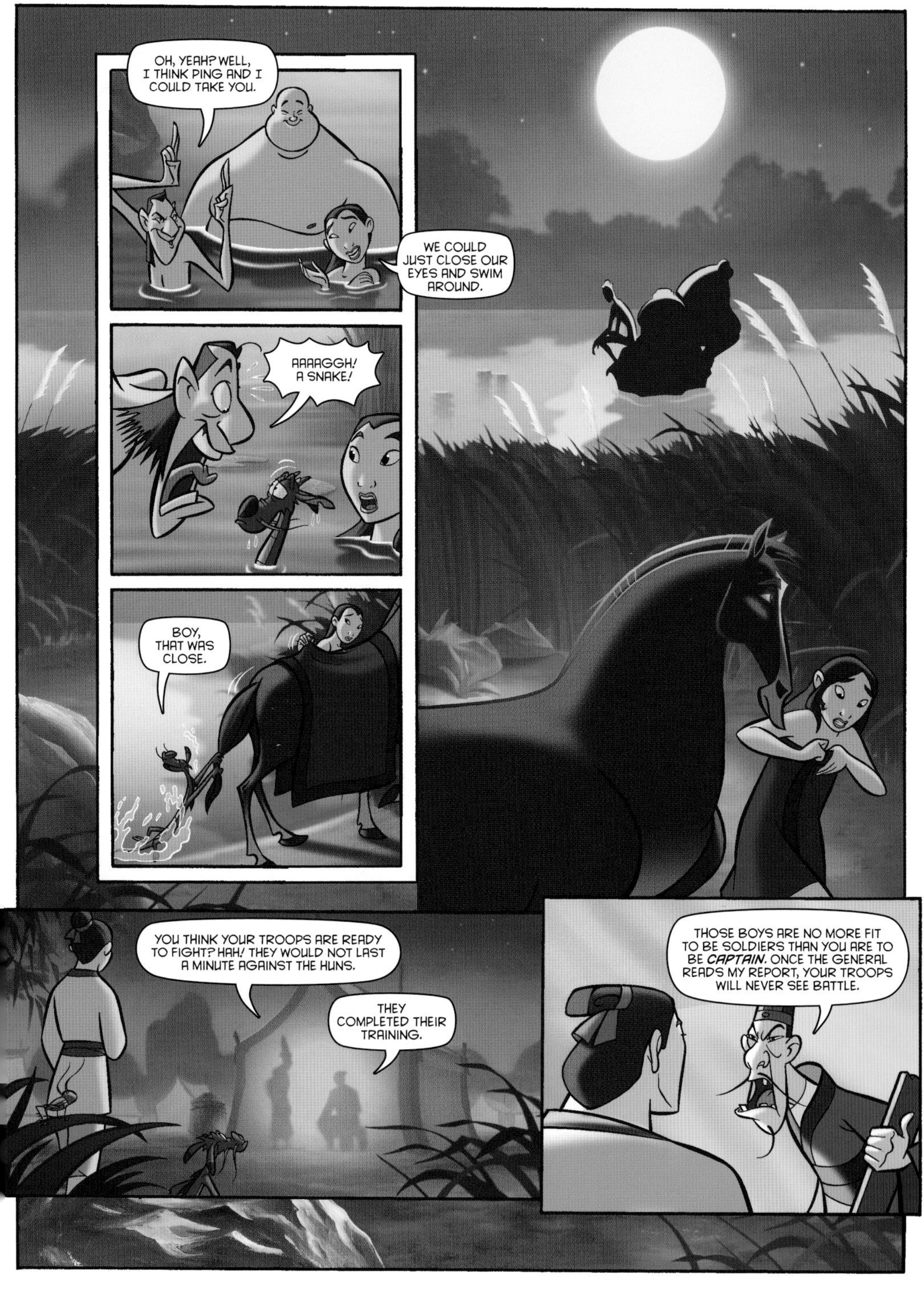
OH, YEAH? WELL, I THINK PING AND I COULD TAKE YOU.
WE COULD JUST CLOSE OUR EYES AND SWIM AROUND.
AAAAGGH! A SNAKE!
BOY, THAT WAS CLOSE.
YOU THINK YOUR TROOPS ARE READY TO FIGHT? HAH! THEY WOULD NOT LAST A MINUTE AGAINST THE HUNS.
THEY COMPLETED THEIR TRAINING.
THOSE BOYS ARE NO MORE FIT TO BE SOLDIERS THAN YOU ARE TO BE CAPTAIN. ONCE THE GENERAL READS MY REPORT, YOUR TROOPS WILL NEVER SEE BATTLE.

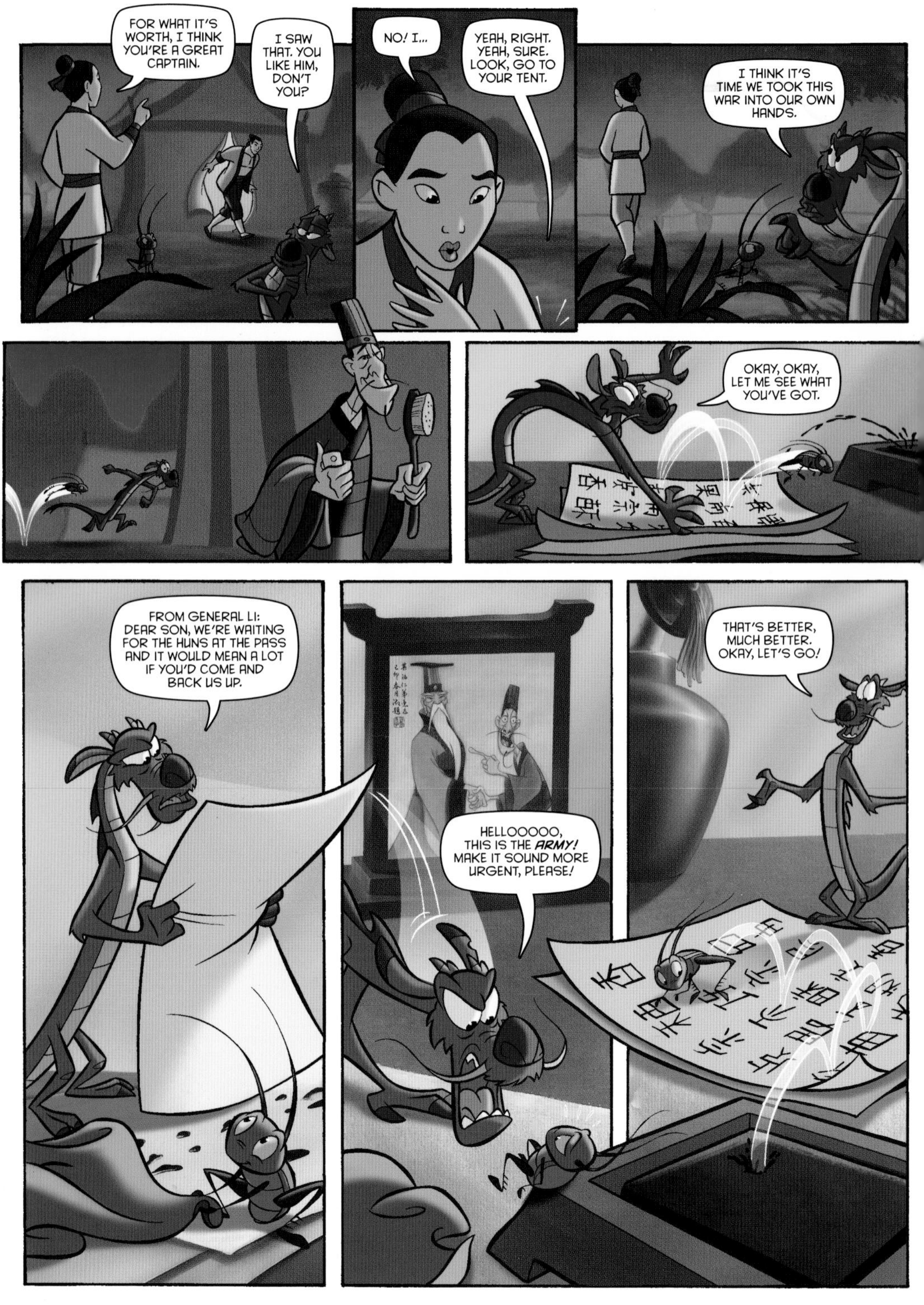
FOR WHAT IT'S WORTH, I THINK YOU'RE A GREAT CAPTAIN.
I SAW THAT. YOU LIKE HIM, DON'T YOU?
NO! I...
YEAH, RIGHT. YEAH, SURE. LOOK, GO TO YOUR TENT.
I THINK IT'S TIME WE TOOK THIS WAR INTO OUR OWN HANDS.
OKAY, OKAY, LET ME SEE WHAT YOU'VE GOT.
FROM GENERAL LI: DEAR SON, WE'RE WAITING FOR THE HUNS AT THE PASS AND IT WOULD MEAN A LOT IF YOU'D COME AND BACK US UP.
HELLOOOOO, THIS IS THE ARMY! MAKE IT SOUND MORE URGENT, PLEASE!
THAT'S BETTER, MUCH BETTER. OKAY, LET'S GO!

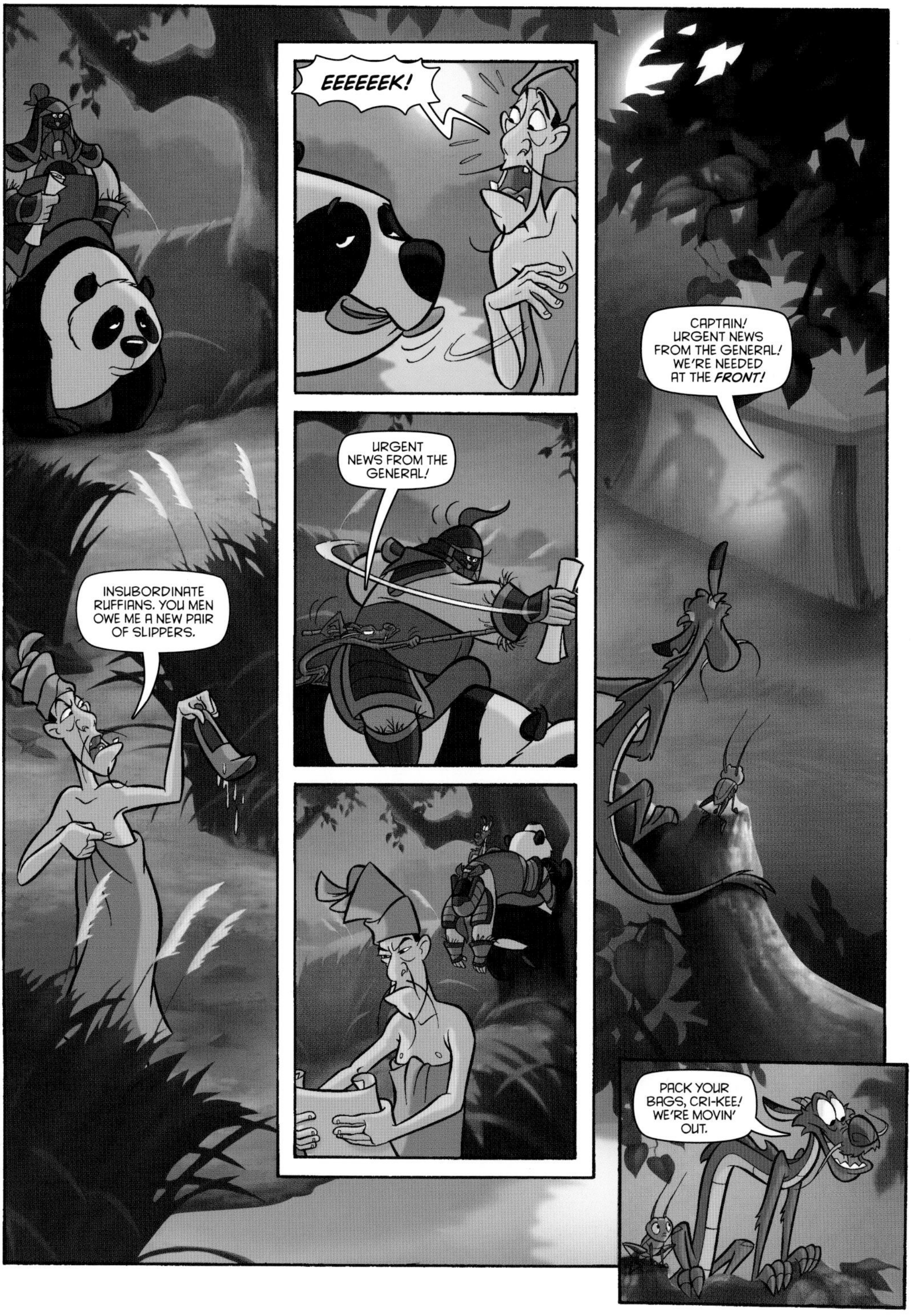

EEEEEEK!
URGENT NEWS FROM THE GENERAL!
INSUBORDINATE RUFFIANS. YOU MEN OWE ME A NEW PAIR OF SLIPPERS.
CAPTAIN! URGENT NEWS FROM THE GENERAL! WE'RE NEEDED AT THE *FRONT!*
PACK YOUR BAGS, CRI-KEE! WE'RE MOVIN' OUT.

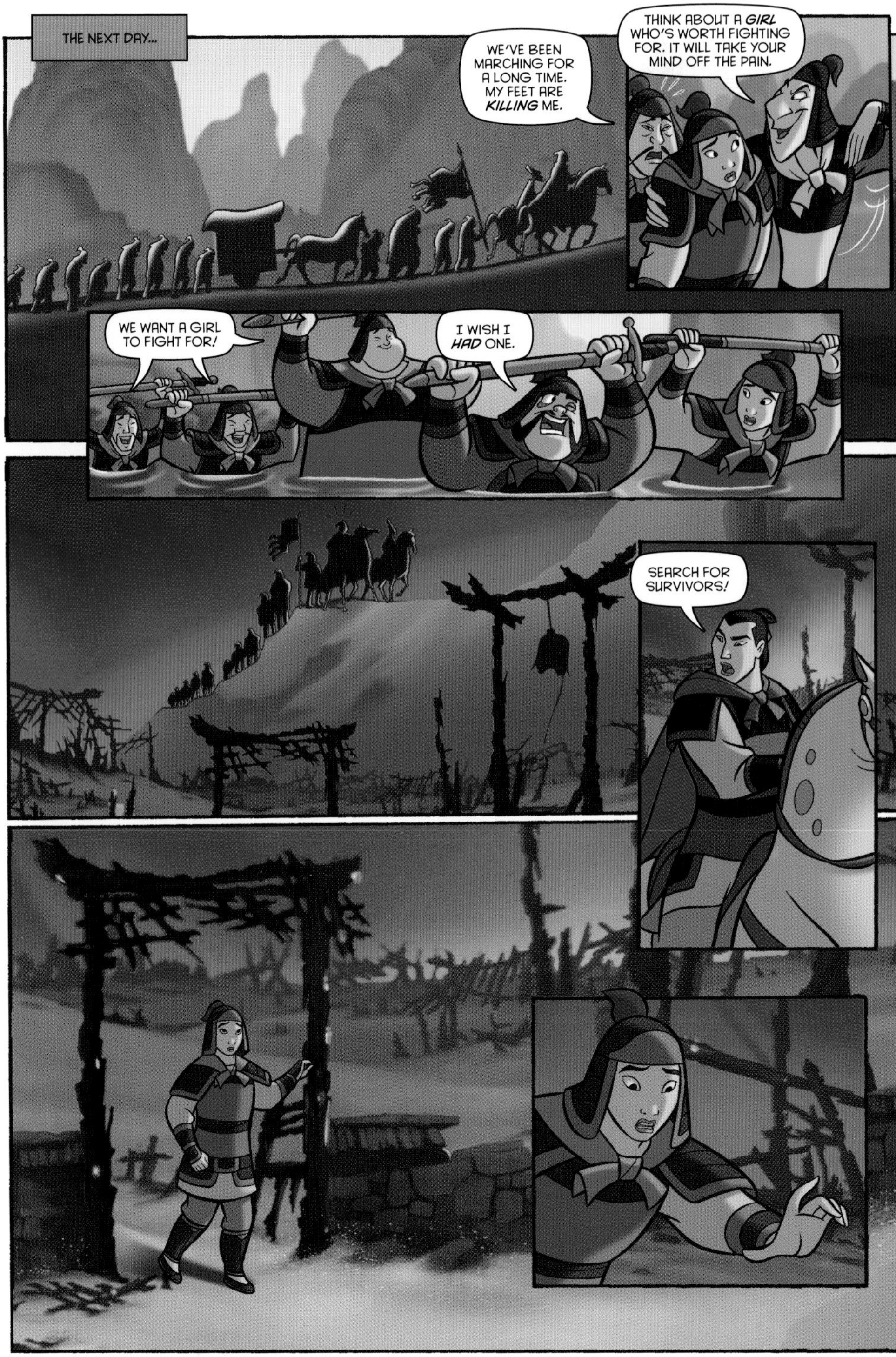
THE NEXT DAY...
WE'VE BEEN MARCHING FOR A LONG TIME. MY FEET ARE KILLING ME.
THINK ABOUT A GIRL WHO'S WORTH FIGHTING FOR. IT WILL TAKE YOUR MIND OFF THE PAIN.
WE WANT A GIRL TO FIGHT FOR!
I WISH I HAD ONE.
SEARCH FOR SURVIVORS!

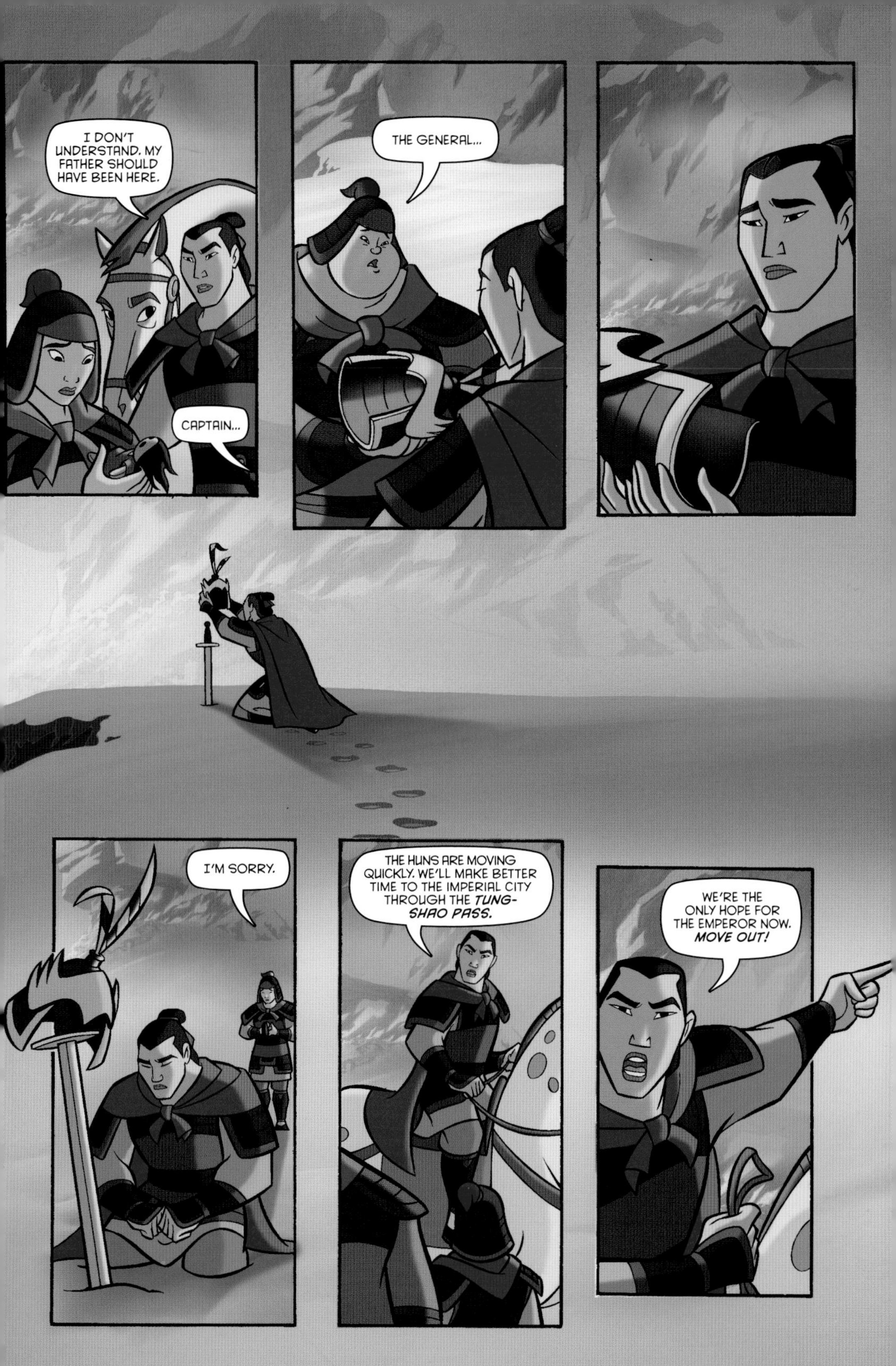
I DON'T UNDERSTAND. MY FATHER SHOULD HAVE BEEN HERE.
CAPTAIN...
THE GENERAL...
I'M SORRY.
THE HUNS ARE MOVING QUICKLY. WE'LL MAKE BETTER TIME TO THE IMPERIAL CITY THROUGH THE *TUNG-SHAO PASS.*
WE'RE THE ONLY HOPE FOR THE EMPEROR NOW. *MOVE OUT!*

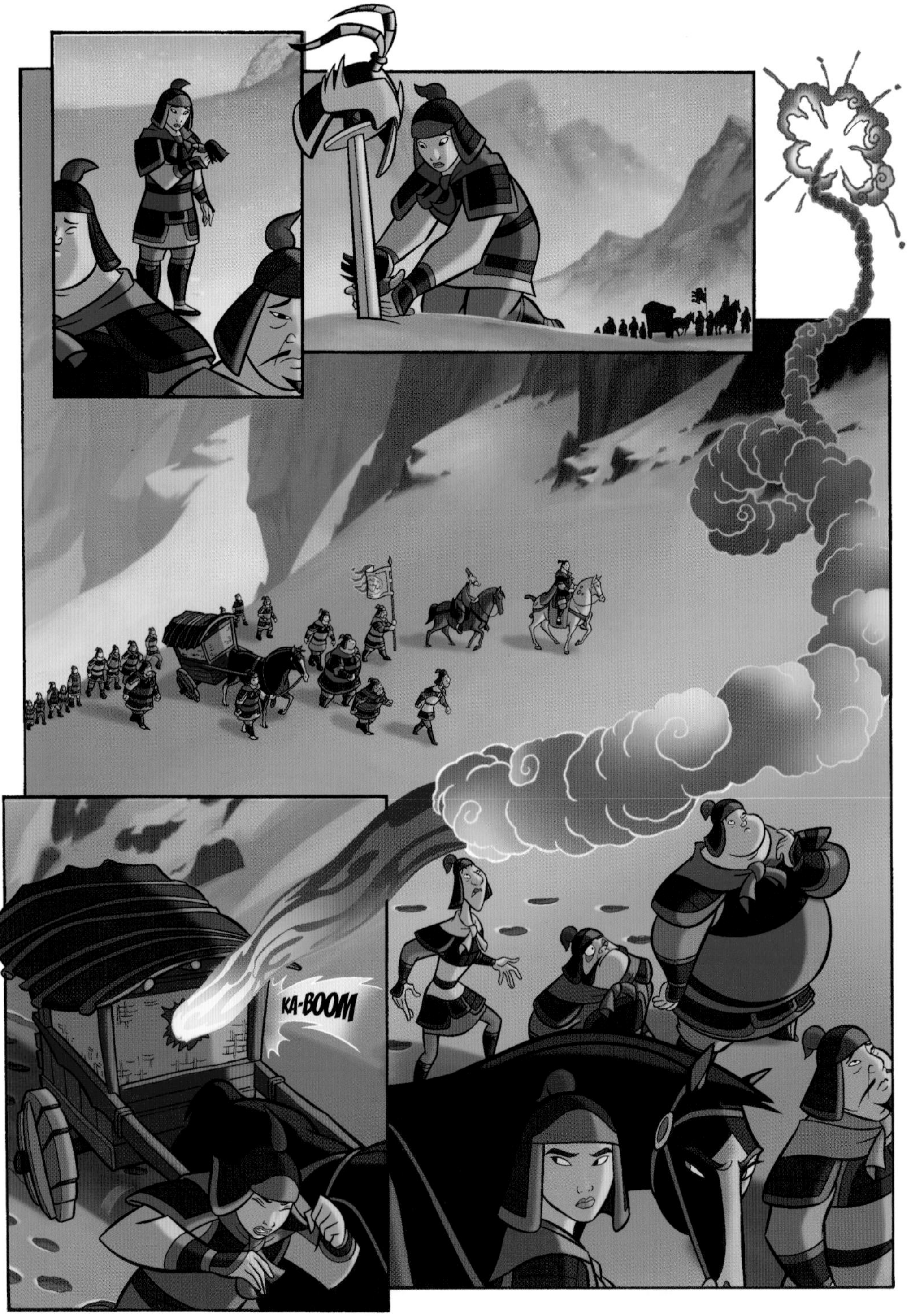
KA-BOOM

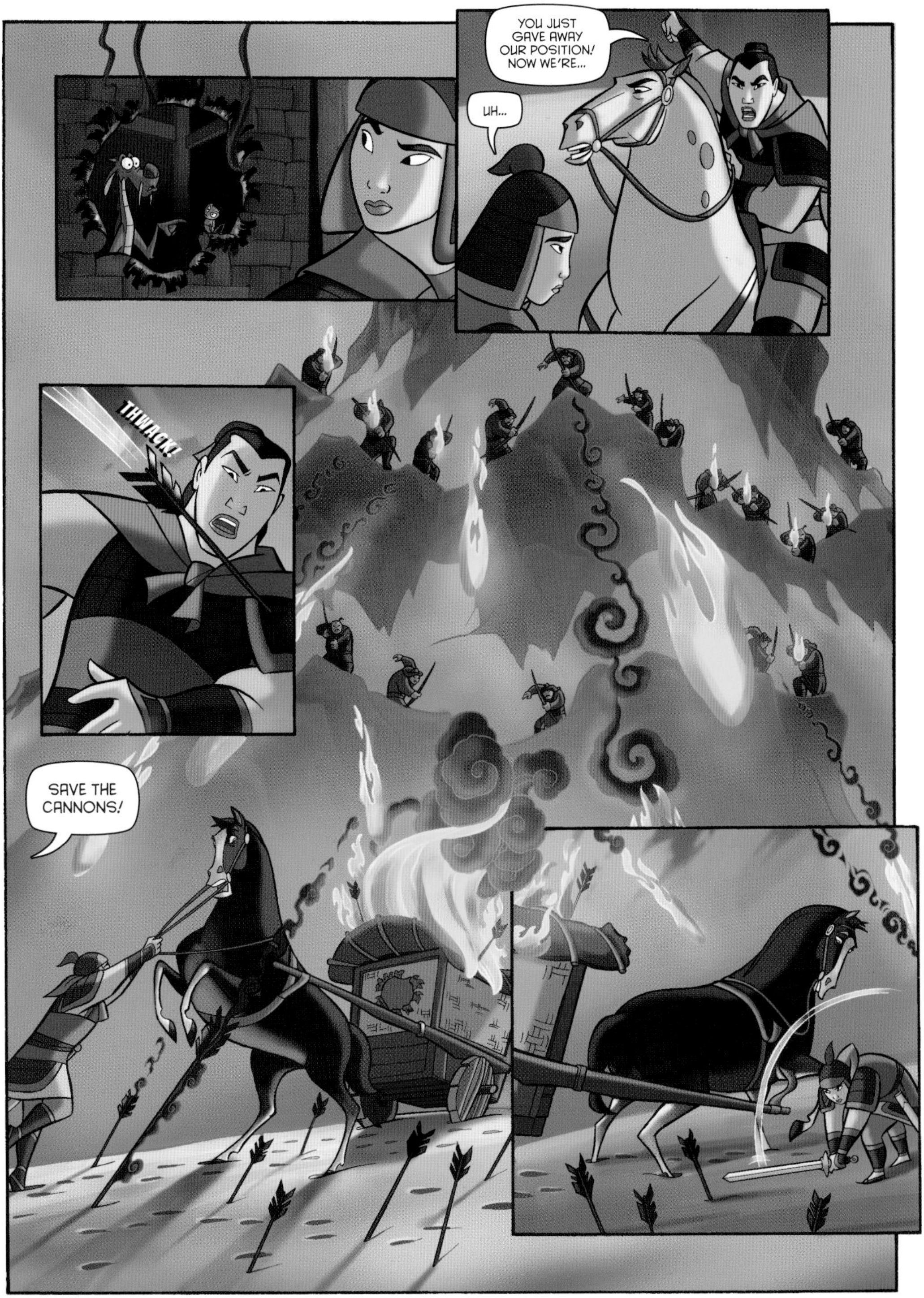
YOU JUST GAVE AWAY OUR POSITION! NOW WE'RE...
UH...
THWACK!
SAVE THE CANNONS!

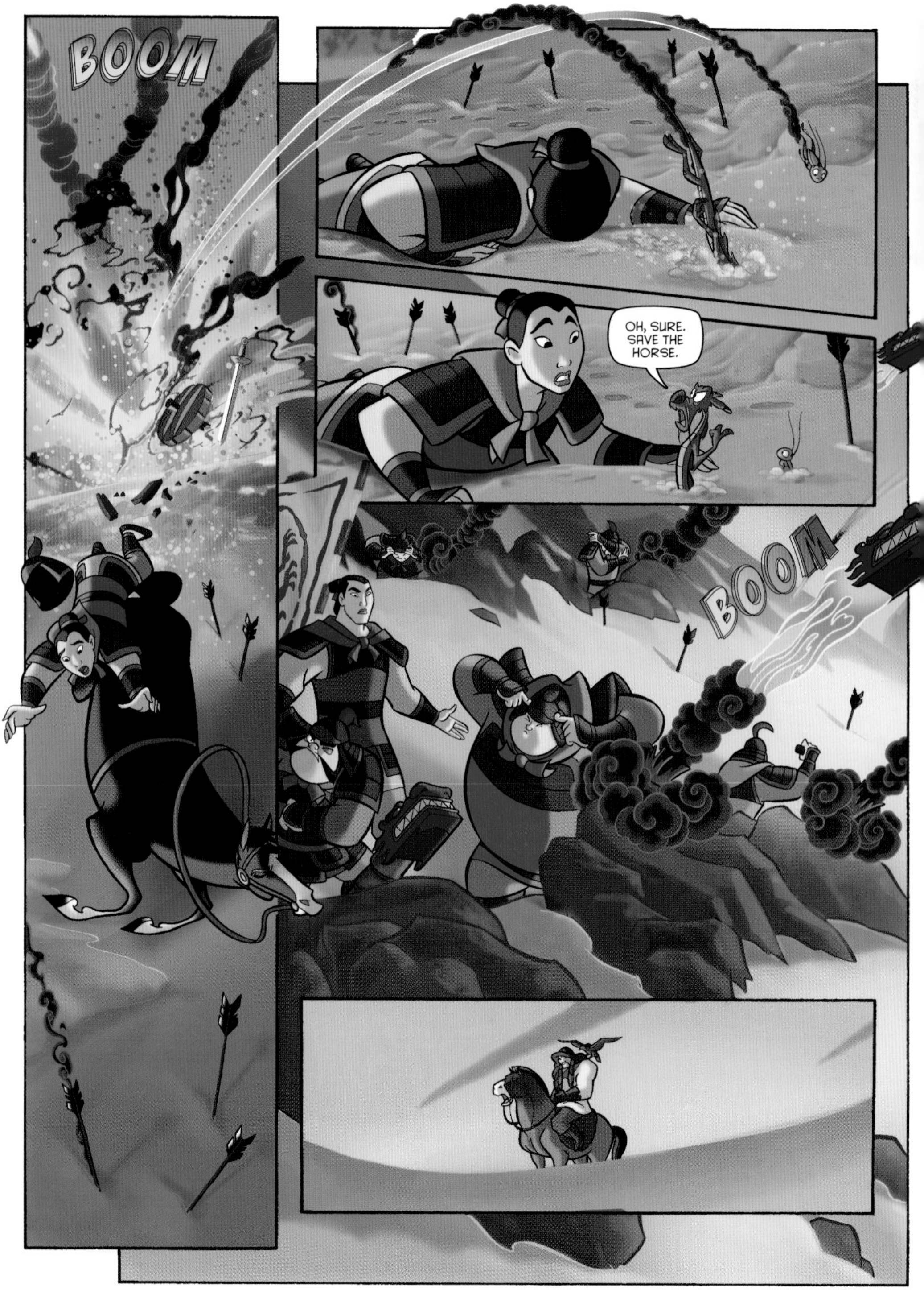
BOOM
OH, SURE. SAVE THE HORSE.
BOOM

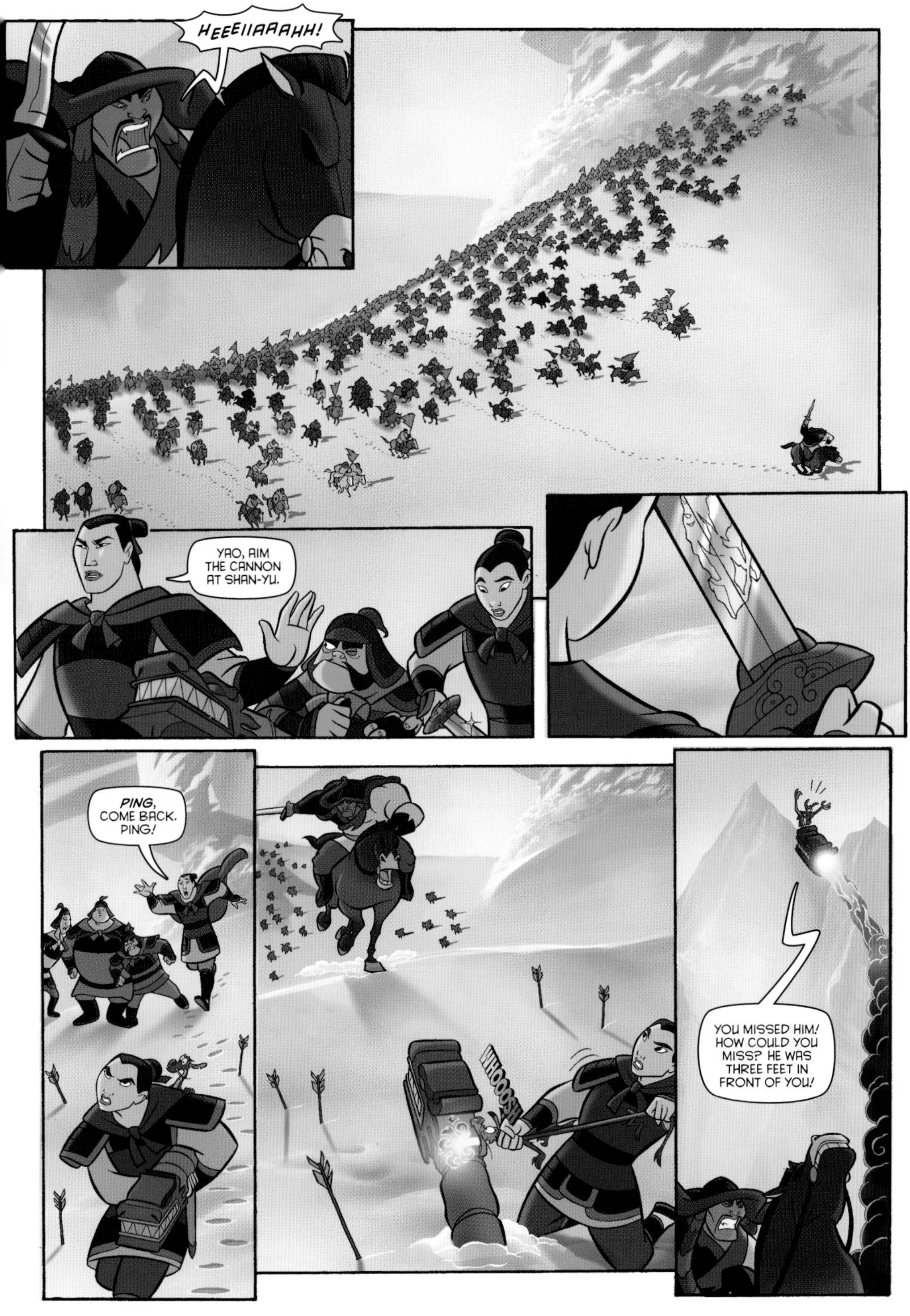
HEEEIIAAAAHH!
YAO, AIM THE CANNON AT SHAN-YU.
PING, COME BACK. PING!
WHOOOSH
YOU MISSED HIM! HOW COULD YOU MISS? HE WAS THREE FEET IN FRONT OF YOU!

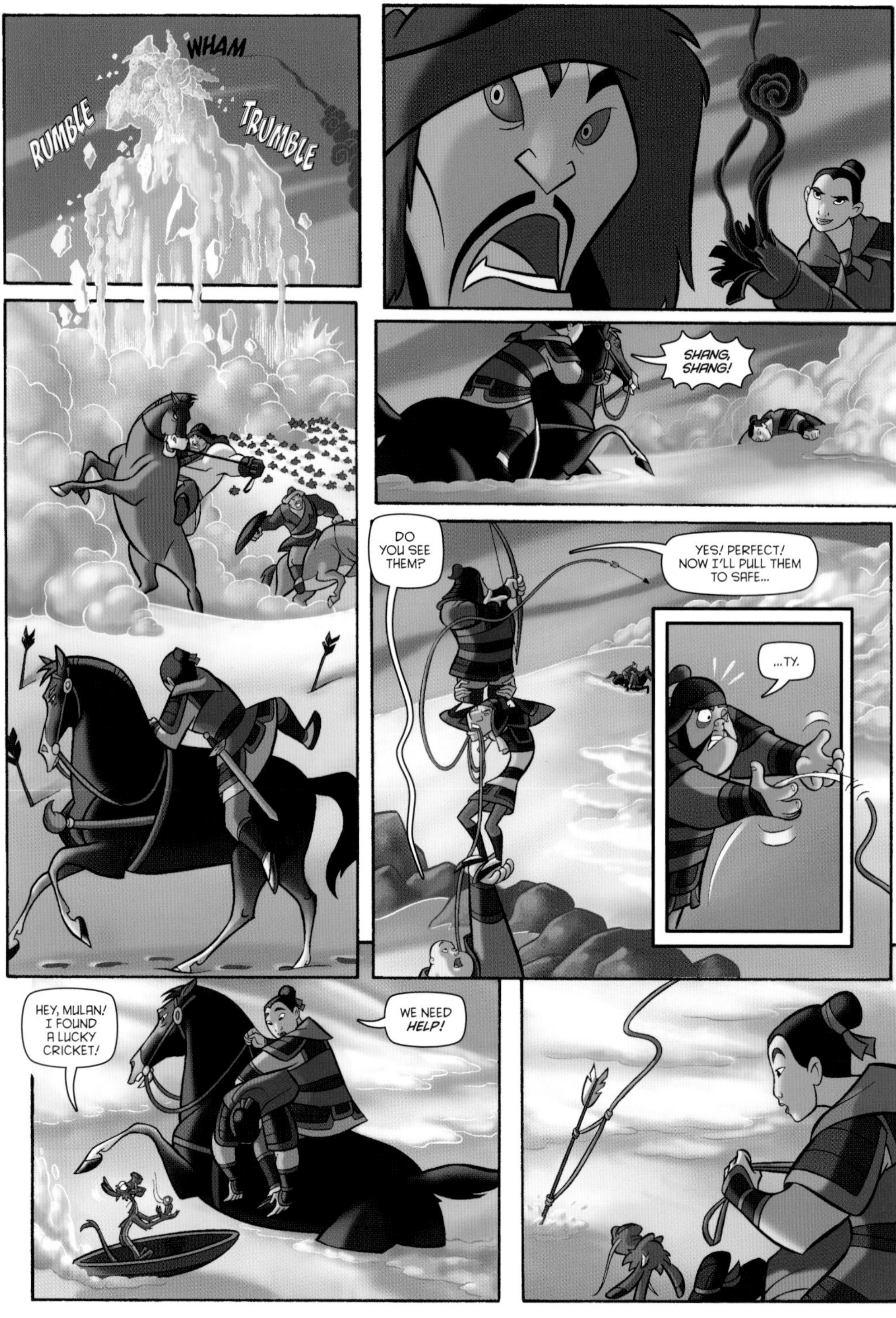
WHAM
RUMBLE
TRUMBLE
SHANG, SHANG!
DO YOU SEE THEM?
YES! PERFECT! NOW I'LL PULL THEM TO SAFE...
...TY.
HEY, MULAN! I FOUND A LUCKY CRICKET!
WE NEED *HELP!*

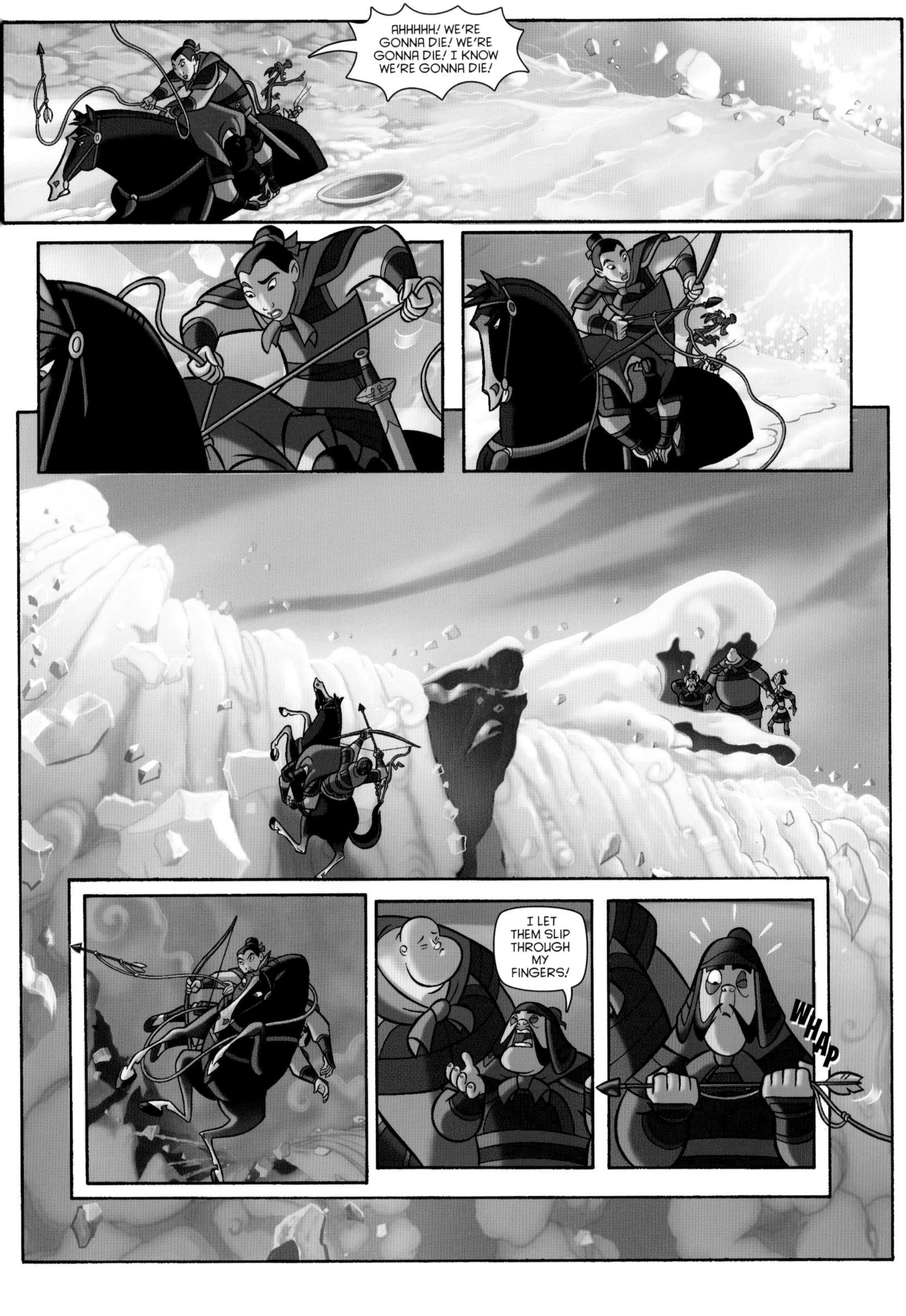
AHHHHH! WE'RE GONNA DIE! WE'RE GONNA DIE! I KNOW WE'RE GONNA DIE!
I LET THEM SLIP THROUGH MY FINGERS!
WHAP

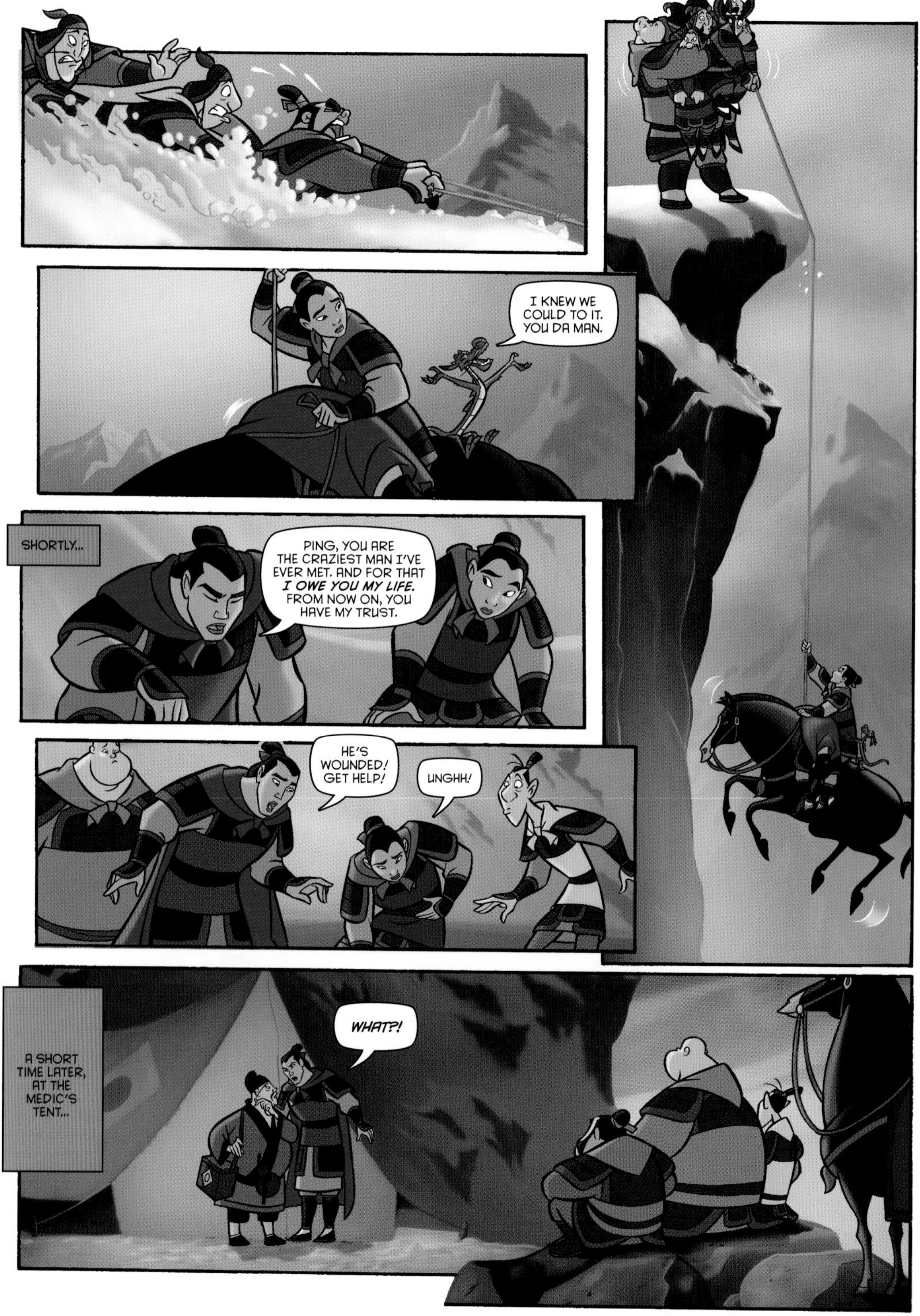
I KNEW WE COULD TO IT. YOU DA MAN.
SHORTLY...
PING, YOU ARE THE CRAZIEST MAN I'VE EVER MET. AND FOR THAT *I OWE YOU MY LIFE.* FROM NOW ON, YOU HAVE MY TRUST.
HE'S WOUNDED! GET HELP!
UNGHH!
A SHORT TIME LATER, AT THE MEDIC'S TENT...
WHAT?!

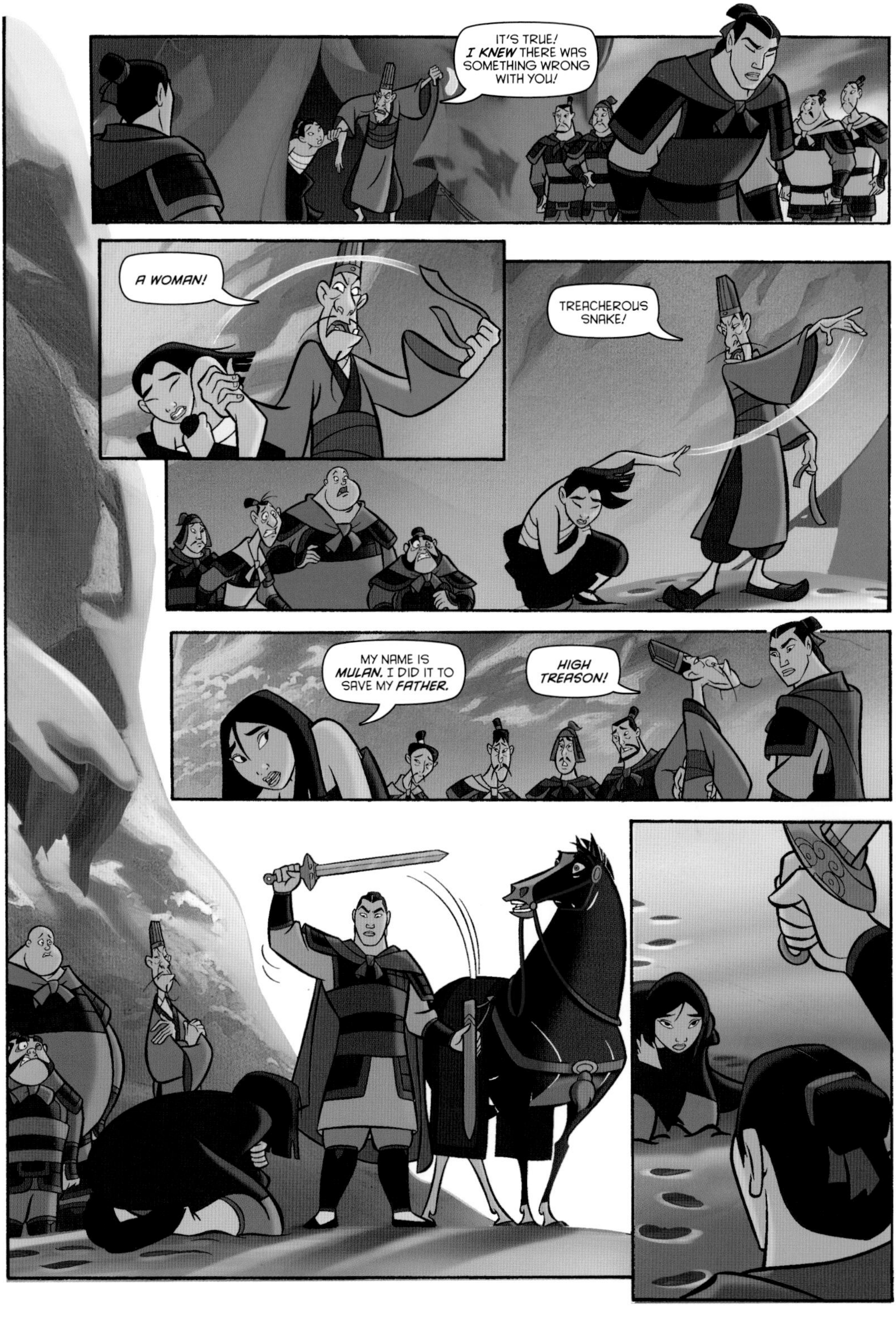
IT'S TRUE! I KNEW THERE WAS SOMETHING WRONG WITH YOU!
A WOMAN!
TREACHEROUS SNAKE!
MY NAME IS MULAN. I DID IT TO SAVE MY FATHER.
HIGH TREASON!

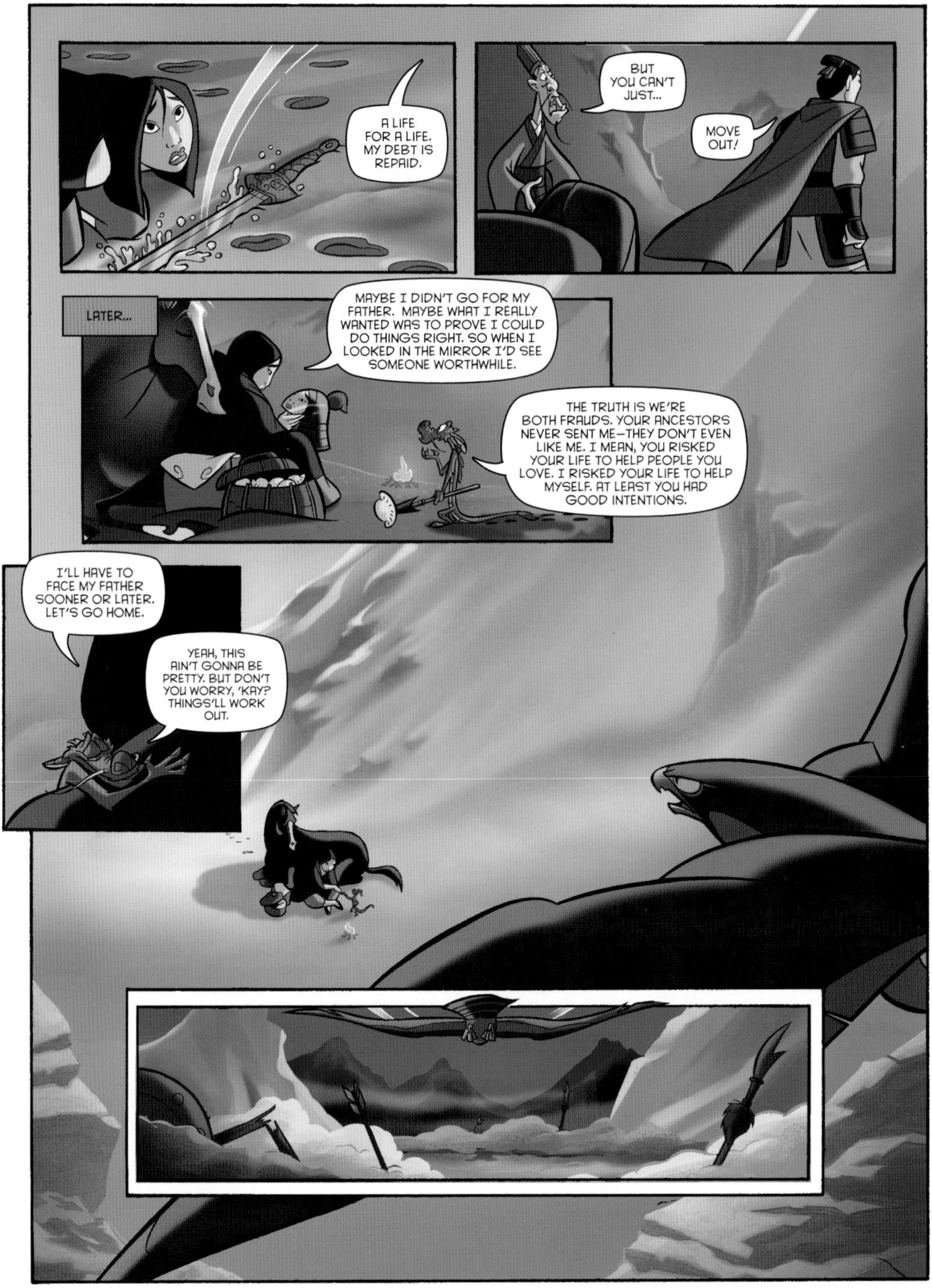
A LIFE FOR A LIFE. MY DEBT IS REPAID.
BUT YOU CAN'T JUST...
MOVE OUT!
LATER...
MAYBE I DIDN'T GO FOR MY FATHER. MAYBE WHAT I REALLY WANTED WAS TO PROVE I COULD DO THINGS RIGHT. SO WHEN I LOOKED IN THE MIRROR I'D SEE SOMEONE WORTHWHILE.
THE TRUTH IS WE'RE BOTH FRAUDS. YOUR ANCESTORS NEVER SENT ME—THEY DON'T EVEN LIKE ME. I MEAN, YOU RISKED YOUR LIFE TO HELP PEOPLE YOU LOVE. I RISKED YOUR LIFE TO HELP MYSELF. AT LEAST YOU HAD GOOD INTENTIONS.
I'LL HAVE TO FACE MY FATHER SOONER OR LATER. LET'S GO HOME.
YEAH, THIS AIN'T GONNA BE PRETTY. BUT DON'T YOU WORRY, 'KAY? THINGS'LL WORK OUT.

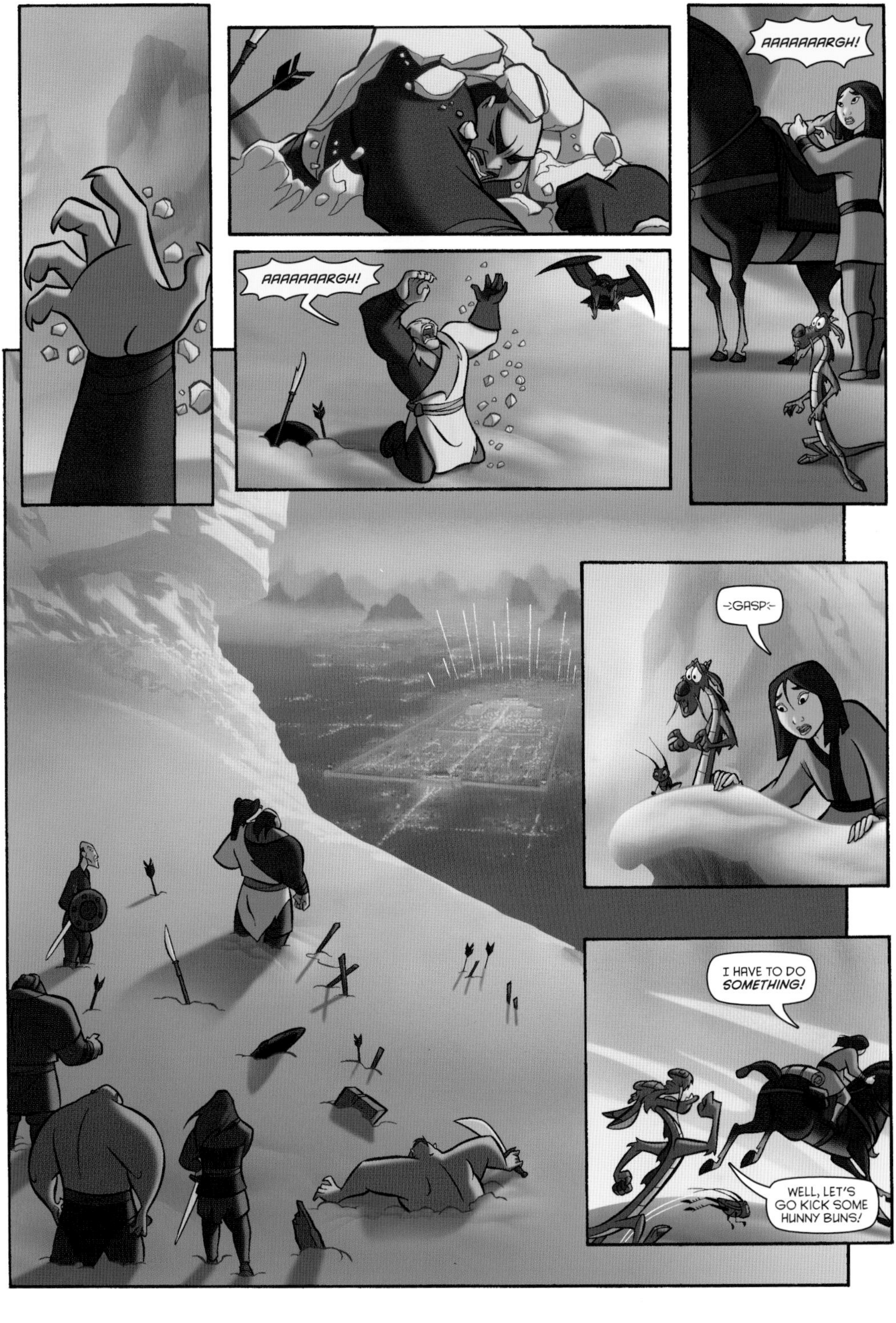
AAAAAAARGH!
AAAAAAARGH!
GASP
I HAVE TO DO SOMETHING!
WELL, LET'S GO KICK SOME HUNNY BUNS!

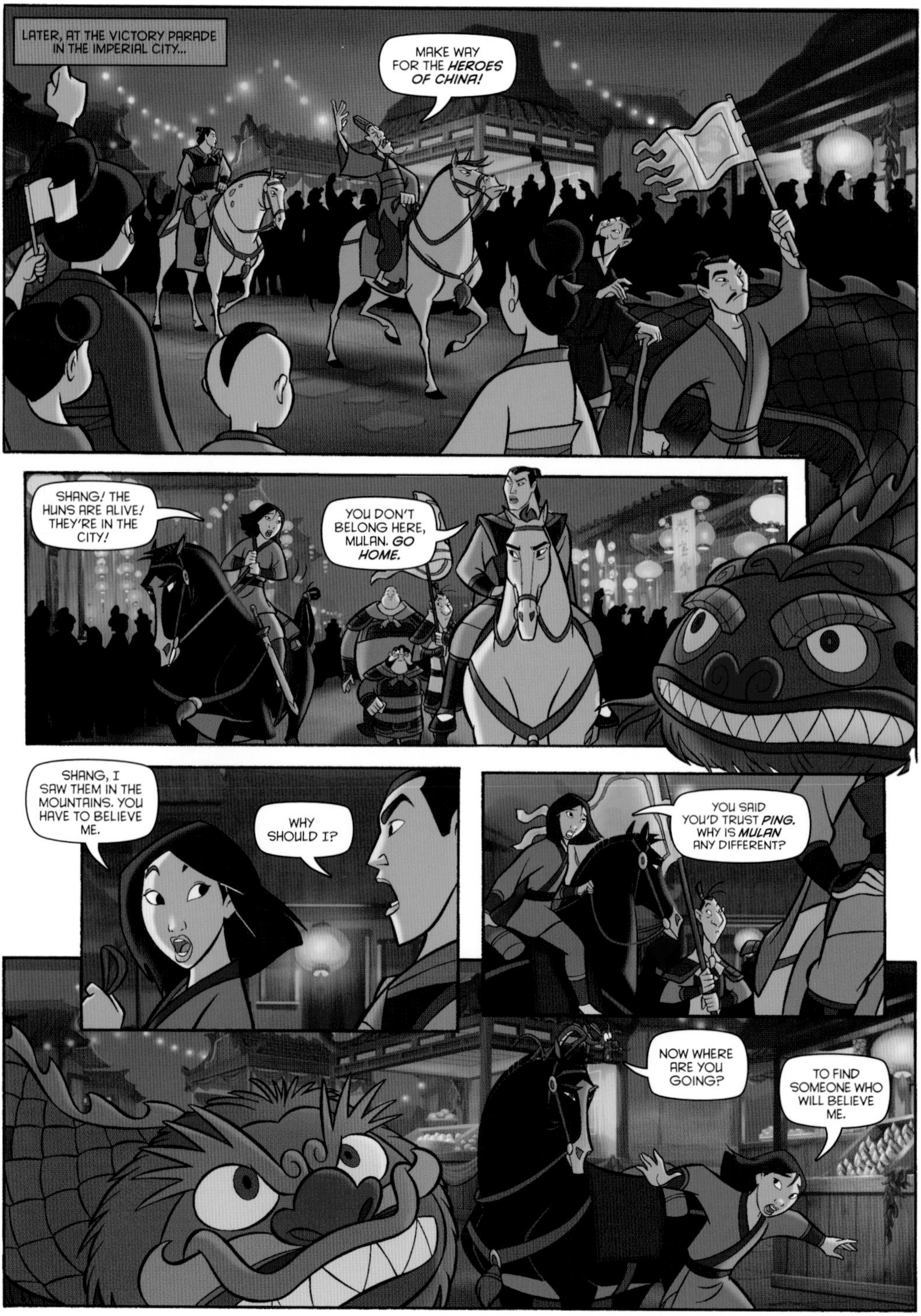
LATER, AT THE VICTORY PARADE IN THE IMPERIAL CITY...
MAKE WAY FOR THE HEROES OF CHINA!
SHANG! THE HUNS ARE ALIVE! THEY'RE IN THE CITY!
YOU DON'T BELONG HERE, MULAN. GO HOME.
SHANG, I SAW THEM IN THE MOUNTAINS. YOU HAVE TO BELIEVE ME.
WHY SHOULD I?
YOU SAID YOU'D TRUST PING. WHY IS MULAN ANY DIFFERENT?
NOW WHERE ARE YOU GOING?
TO FIND SOMEONE WHO WILL BELIEVE ME.

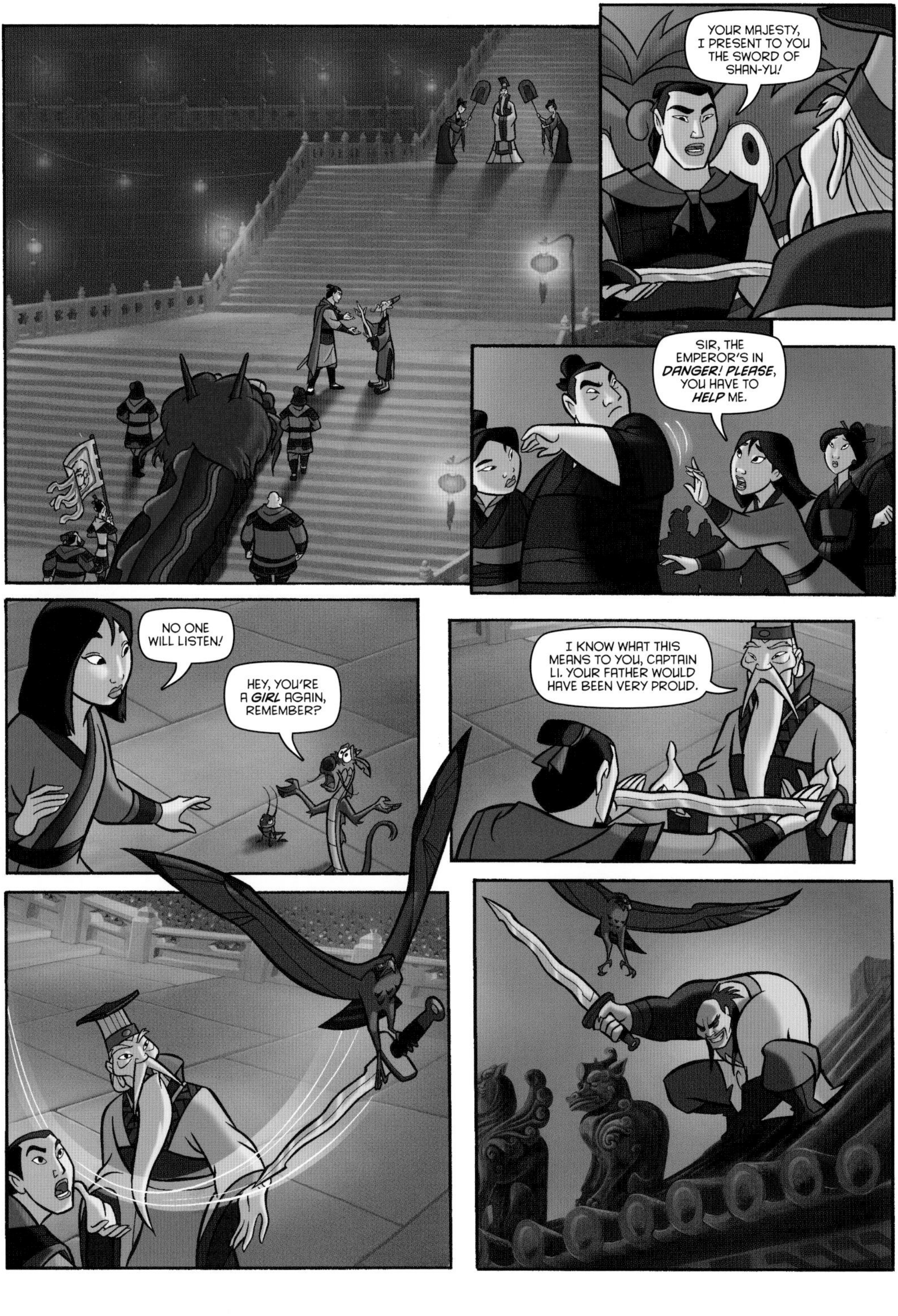
YOUR MAJESTY, I PRESENT TO YOU THE SWORD OF SHAN-YU!
SIR, THE EMPEROR'S IN DANGER! PLEASE, YOU HAVE TO HELP ME.
NO ONE WILL LISTEN!
HEY, YOU'RE A GIRL AGAIN, REMEMBER?
I KNOW WHAT THIS MEANS TO YOU, CAPTAIN LI. YOUR FATHER WOULD HAVE BEEN VERY PROUD.

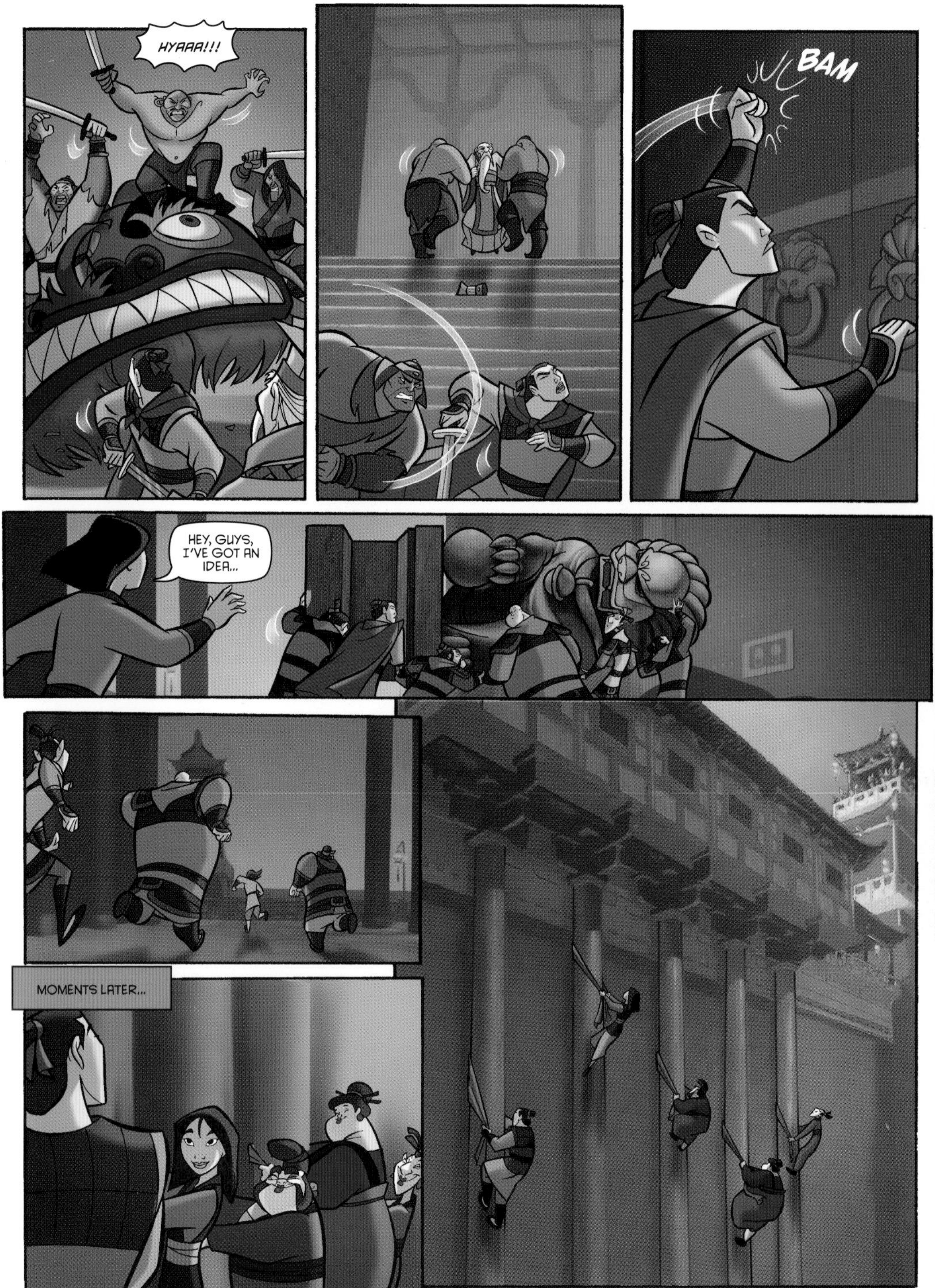
HYAAA!!!
BAM
HEY, GUYS, I'VE GOT AN IDEA...
MOMENTS LATER...

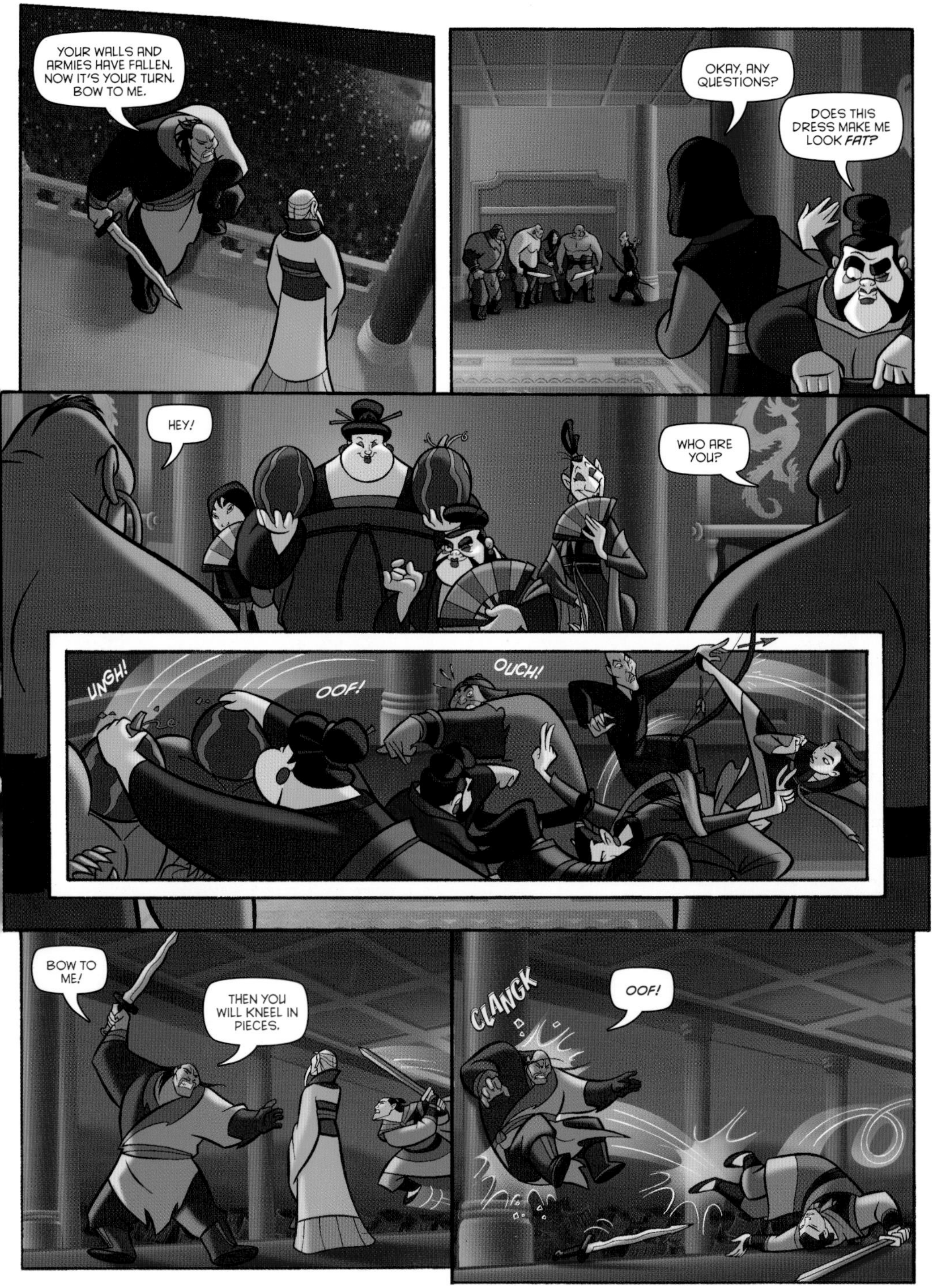
YOUR WALLS AND ARMIES HAVE FALLEN. NOW IT'S YOUR TURN. BOW TO ME.
OKAY, ANY QUESTIONS?
DOES THIS DRESS MAKE ME LOOK *FAT?*
HEY!
WHO ARE YOU?
UNGH!
OOF!
OUCH!
BOW TO ME!
THEN YOU WILL KNEEL IN PIECES.
CLANGK
OOF!

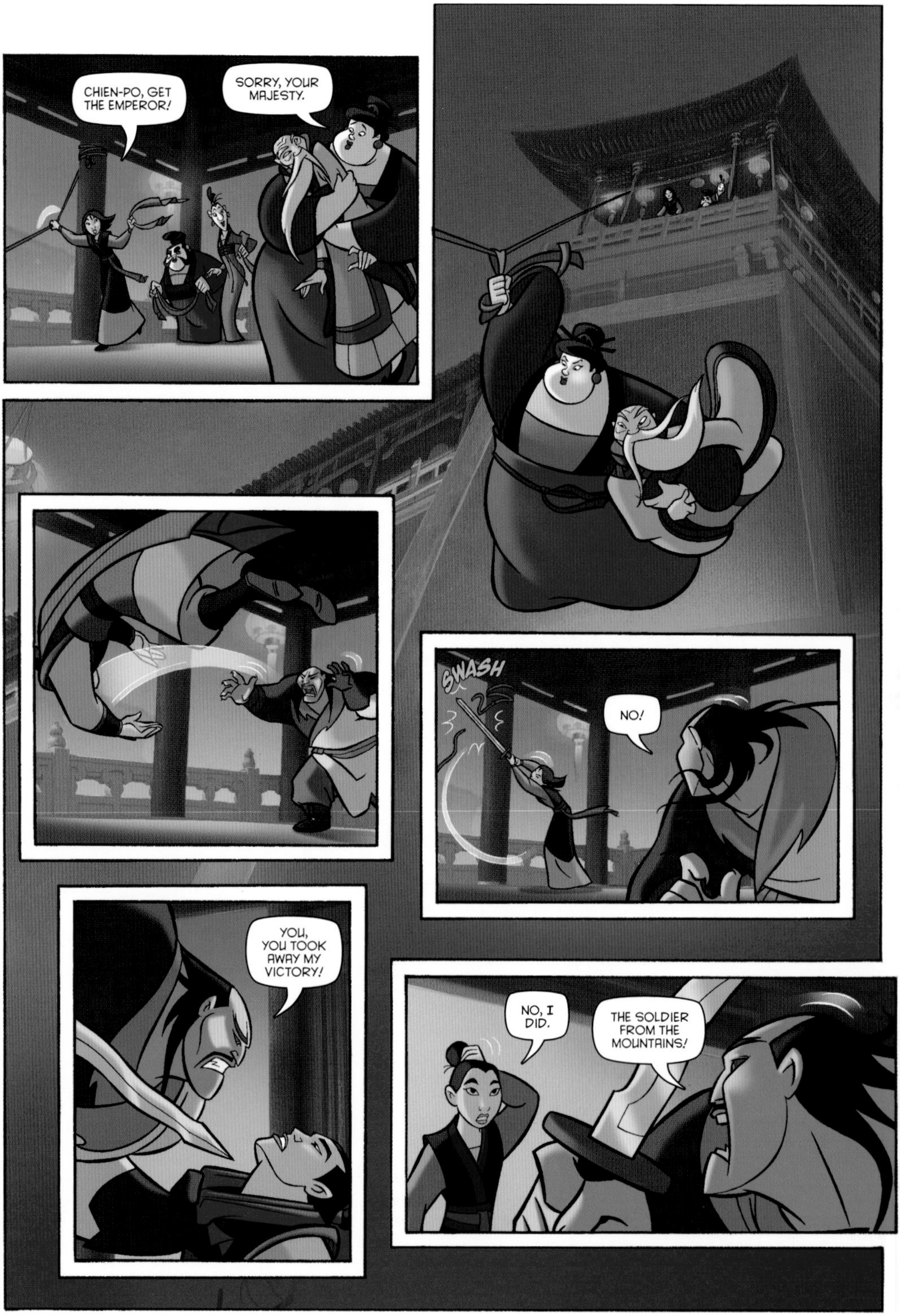
CHIEN-PO, GET THE EMPEROR!
SORRY, YOUR MAJESTY.
SWASH
NO!
YOU, YOU TOOK AWAY MY VICTORY!
NO, I DID.
THE SOLDIER FROM THE MOUNTAINS!

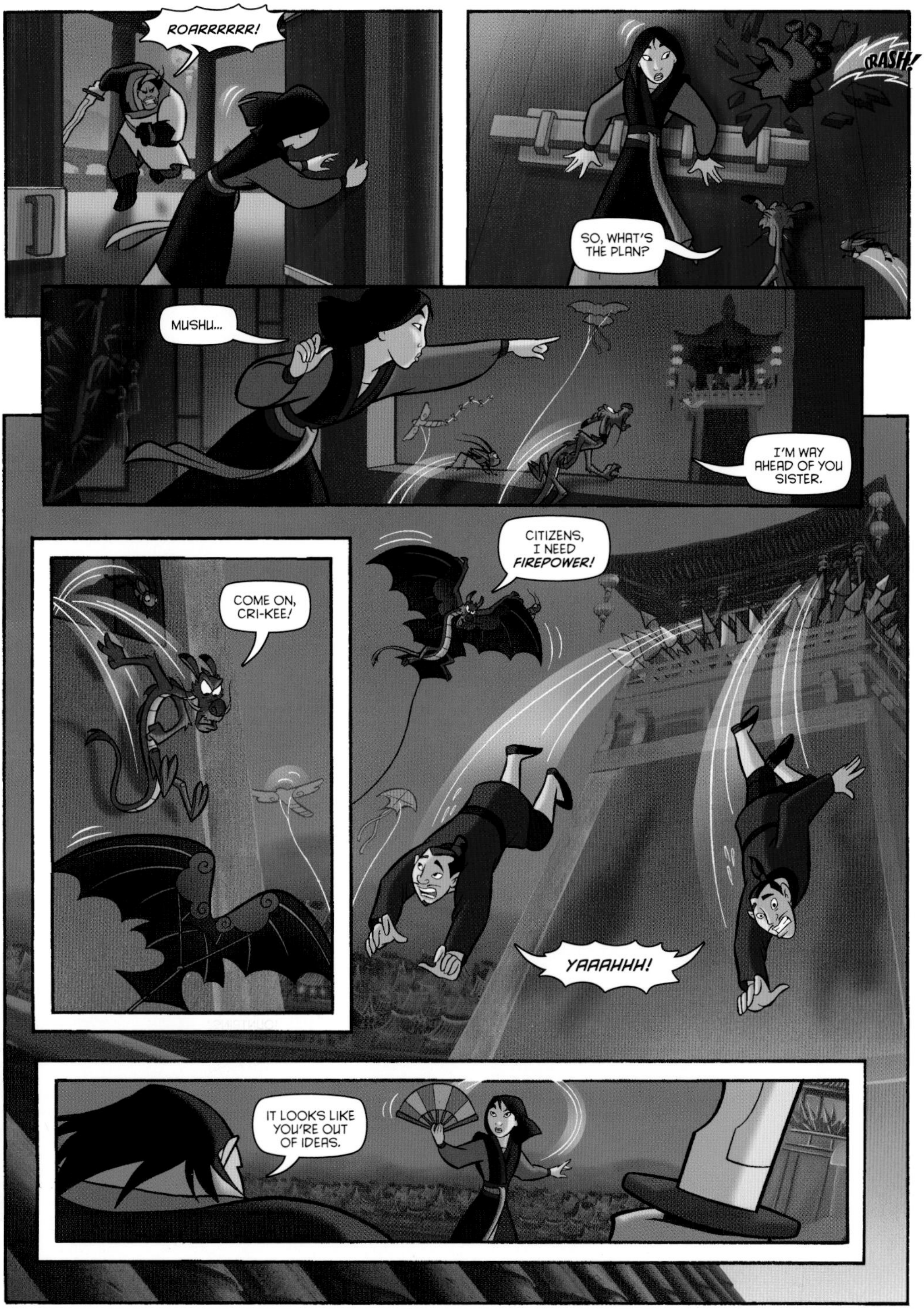
ROARRRRRR!
CRASH!
SO, WHAT'S THE PLAN?
MUSHU...
I'M WAY AHEAD OF YOU SISTER.
COME ON, CRI-KEE!
CITIZENS, I NEED FIREPOWER!
YAAAHHH!
IT LOOKS LIKE YOU'RE OUT OF IDEAS.

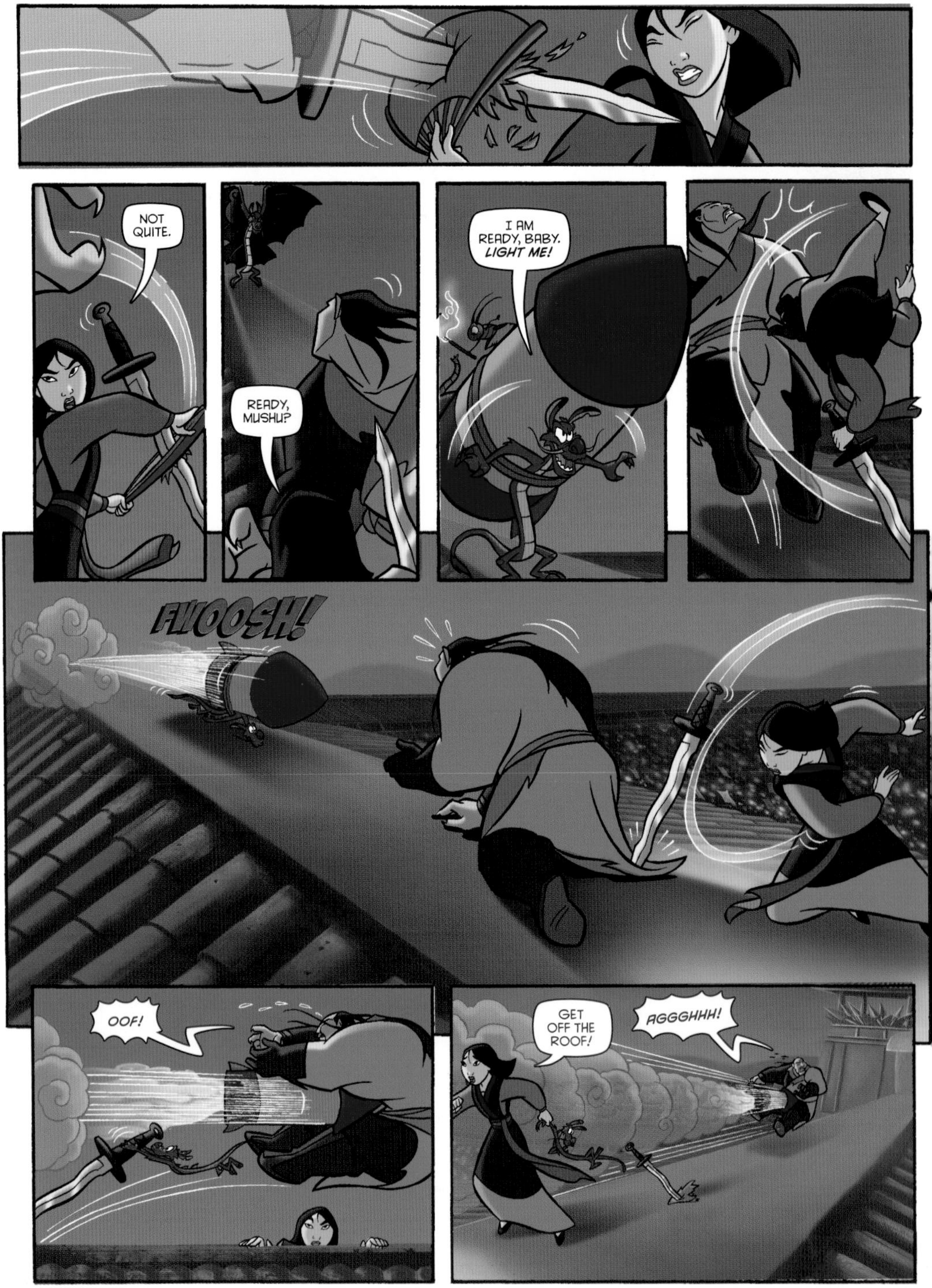
NOT QUITE.
READY, MUSHU?
I AM READY, BABY. LIGHT ME!
FWOOSH!
OOF!
GET OFF THE ROOF!
AGGGHHH!

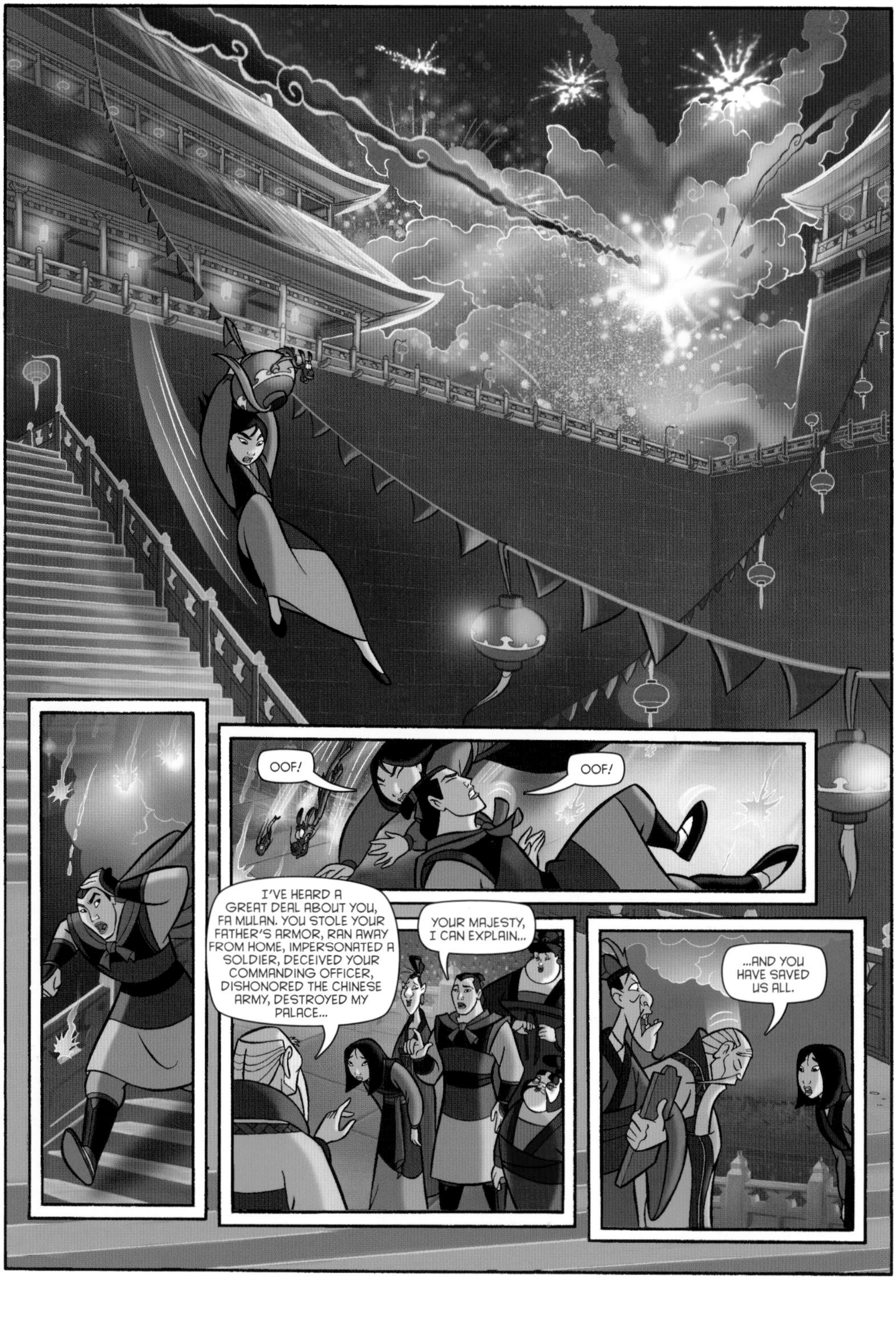
OOF!
OOF!
I'VE HEARD A GREAT DEAL ABOUT YOU, FA MULAN. YOU STOLE YOUR FATHER'S ARMOR, RAN AWAY FROM HOME, IMPERSONATED A SOLDIER, DECEIVED YOUR COMMANDING OFFICER, DISHONORED THE CHINESE ARMY, DESTROYED MY PALACE...
YOUR MAJESTY, I CAN EXPLAIN...
...AND YOU HAVE SAVED US ALL.

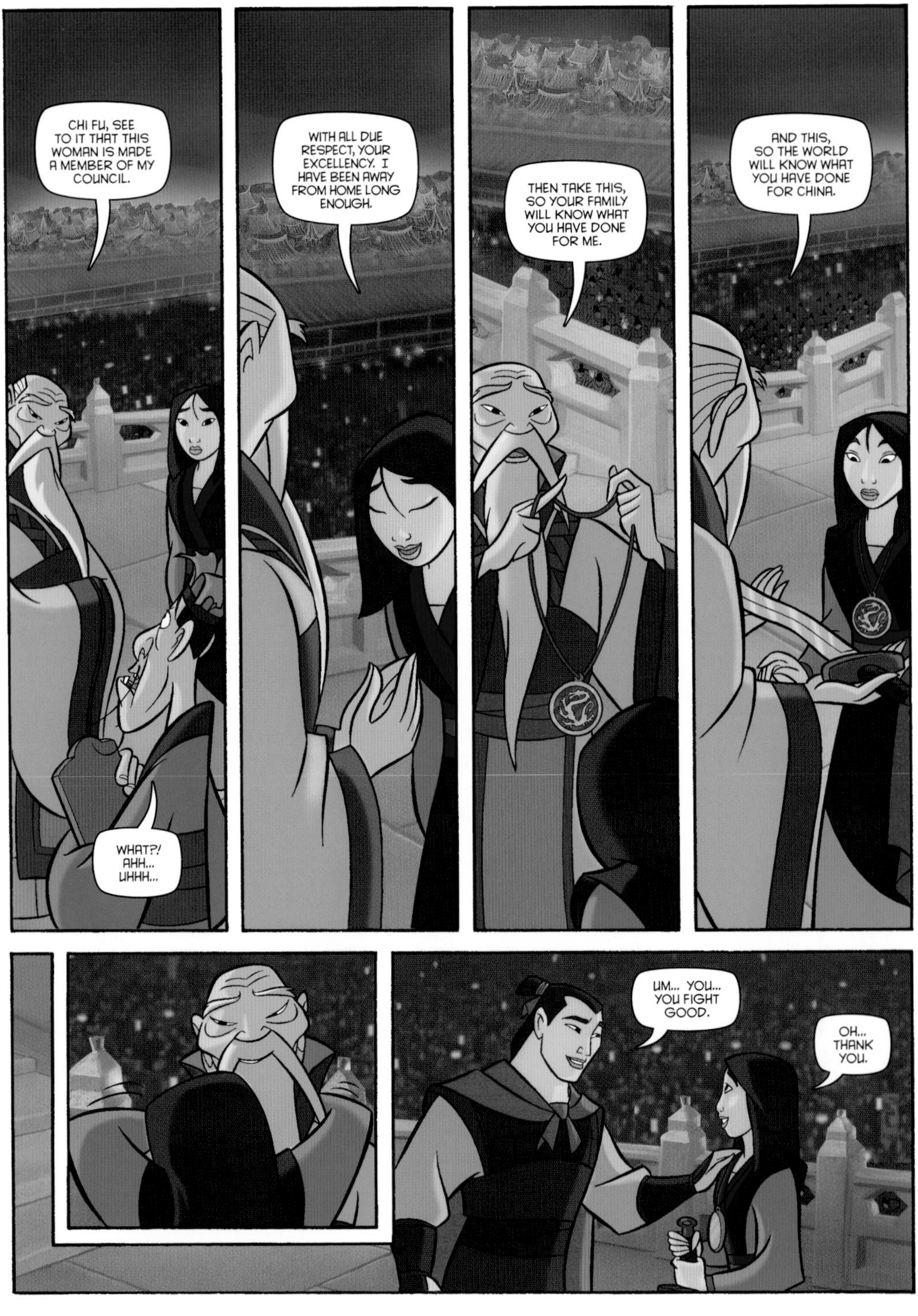
CHI FU, SEE TO IT THAT THIS WOMAN IS MADE A MEMBER OF MY COUNCIL.
WHAT?! AHH... UHHH...
WITH ALL DUE RESPECT, YOUR EXCELLENCY. I HAVE BEEN AWAY FROM HOME LONG ENOUGH.
THEN TAKE THIS, SO YOUR FAMILY WILL KNOW WHAT YOU HAVE DONE FOR ME.
AND THIS, SO THE WORLD WILL KNOW WHAT YOU HAVE DONE FOR CHINA.
UM... YOU... YOU FIGHT GOOD.
OH... THANK YOU.

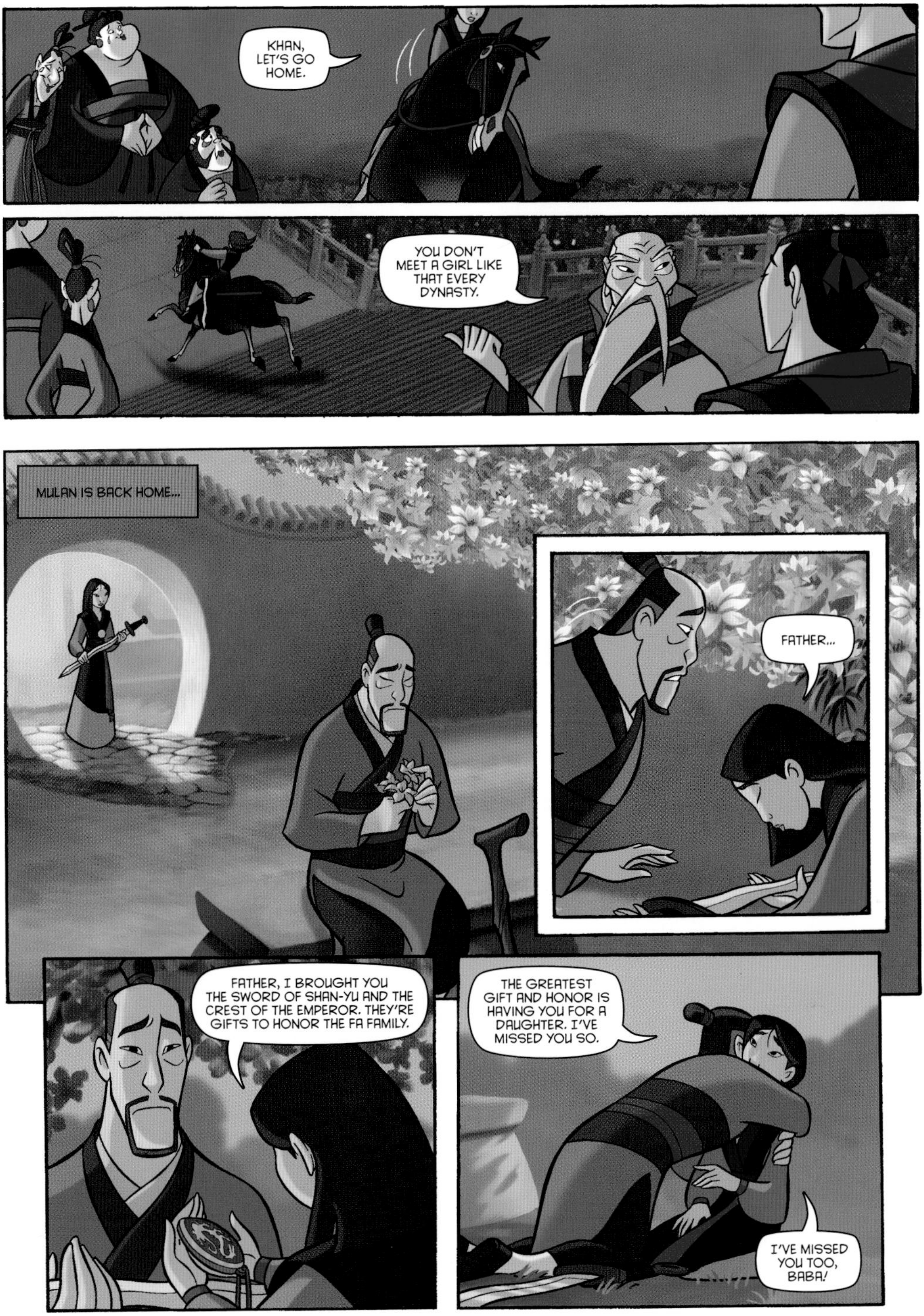

KHAN, LET'S GO HOME.
YOU DON'T MEET A GIRL LIKE THAT EVERY DYNASTY.
MULAN IS BACK HOME...
FATHER...
FATHER, I BROUGHT YOU THE SWORD OF SHAN-YU AND THE CREST OF THE EMPEROR. THEY'RE GIFTS TO HONOR THE FA FAMILY.
THE GREATEST GIFT AND HONOR IS HAVING YOU FOR A DAUGHTER. I'VE MISSED YOU SO.
I'VE MISSED YOU TOO, BABA!

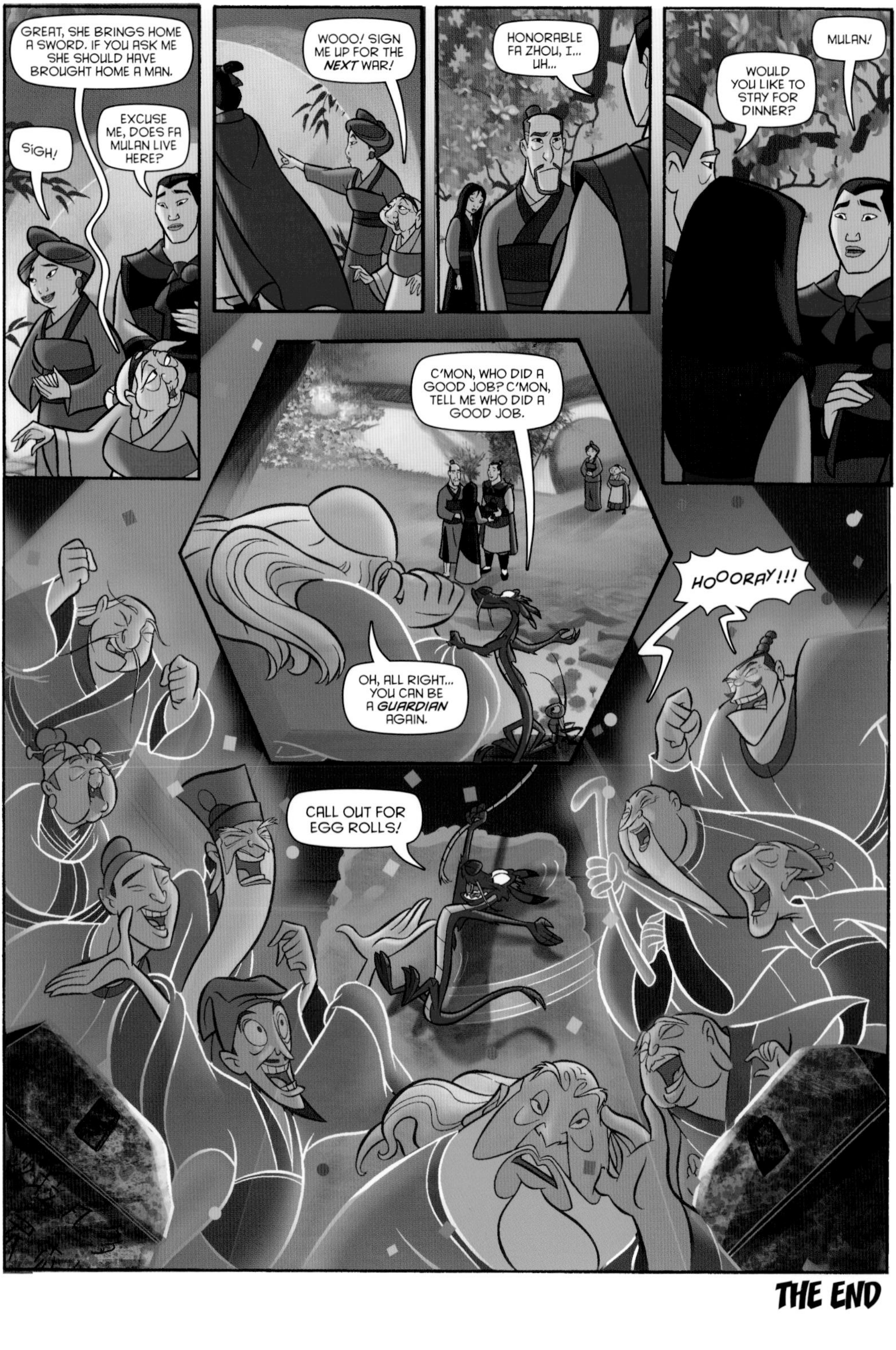
GREAT, SHE BRINGS HOME A SWORD. IF YOU ASK ME SHE SHOULD HAVE BROUGHT HOME A MAN.
SIGH!
EXCUSE ME, DOES FA MULAN LIVE HERE?
WOOO! SIGN ME UP FOR THE NEXT WAR!
HONORABLE FA ZHOU, I... UH...
WOULD YOU LIKE TO STAY FOR DINNER?
MULAN!
C'MON, WHO DID A GOOD JOB? C'MON, TELL ME WHO DID A GOOD JOB.
OH, ALL RIGHT... YOU CAN BE A GUARDIAN AGAIN.
HOOORAY!!!
CALL OUT FOR EGG ROLLS!

THE END

"A single grain of rice can tip the scale;
one man may be the difference
between victory and defeat."

Emperor

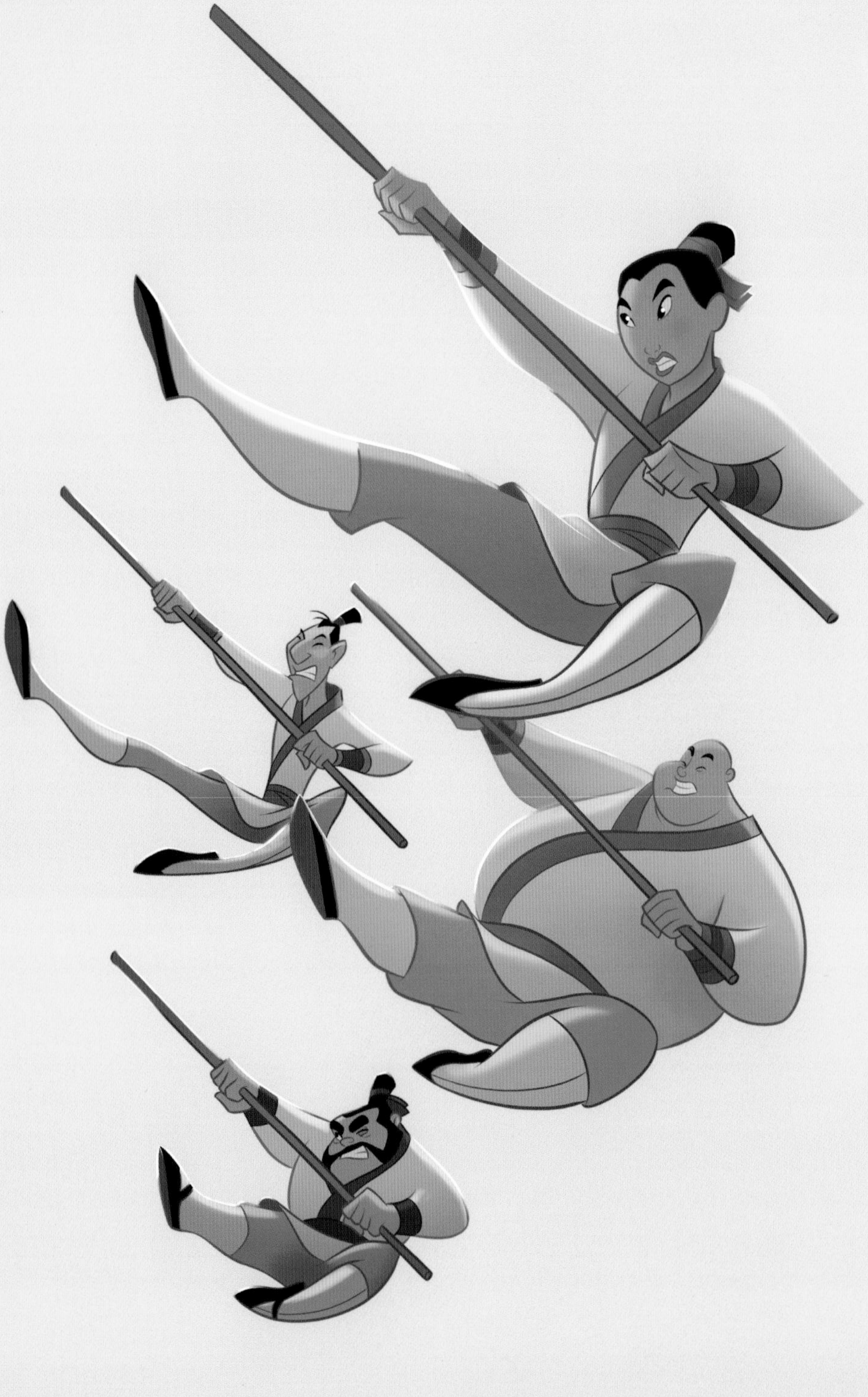

MULAN

—————

MEMORIES

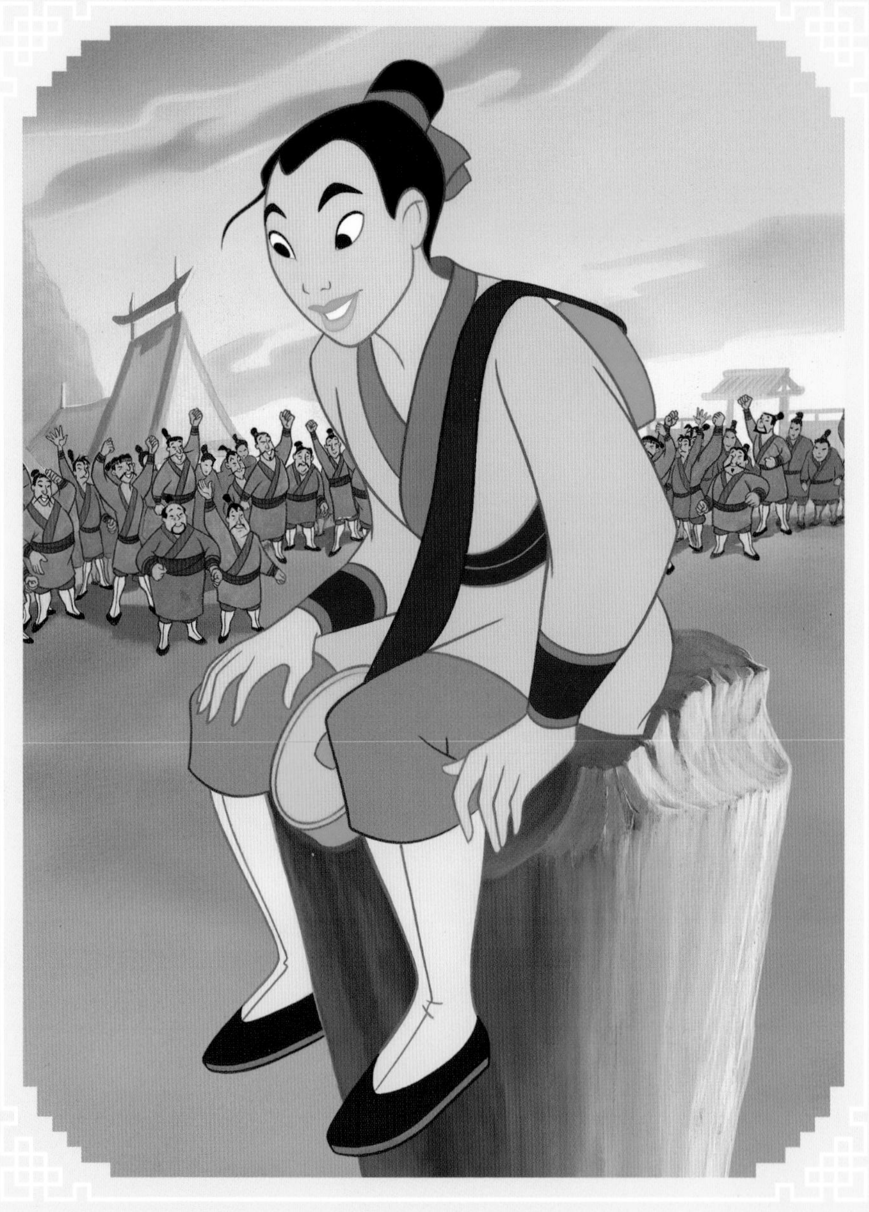

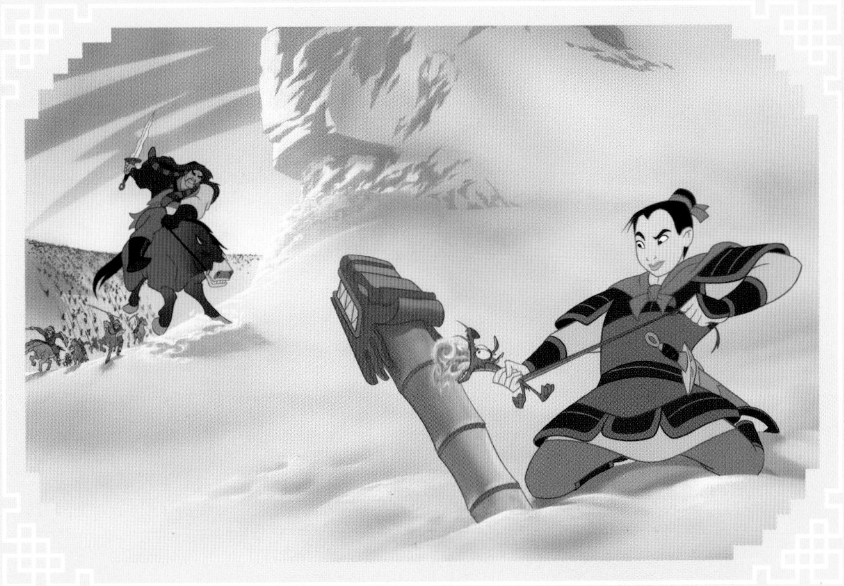

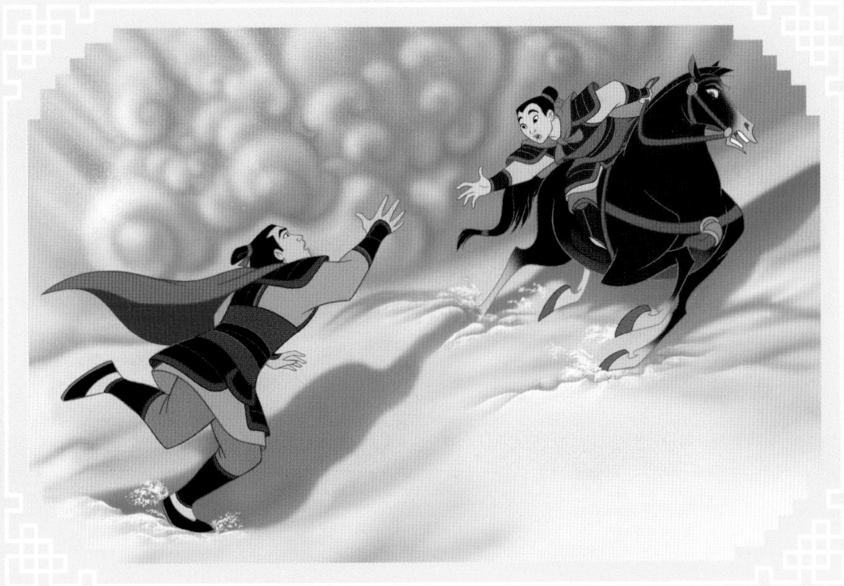

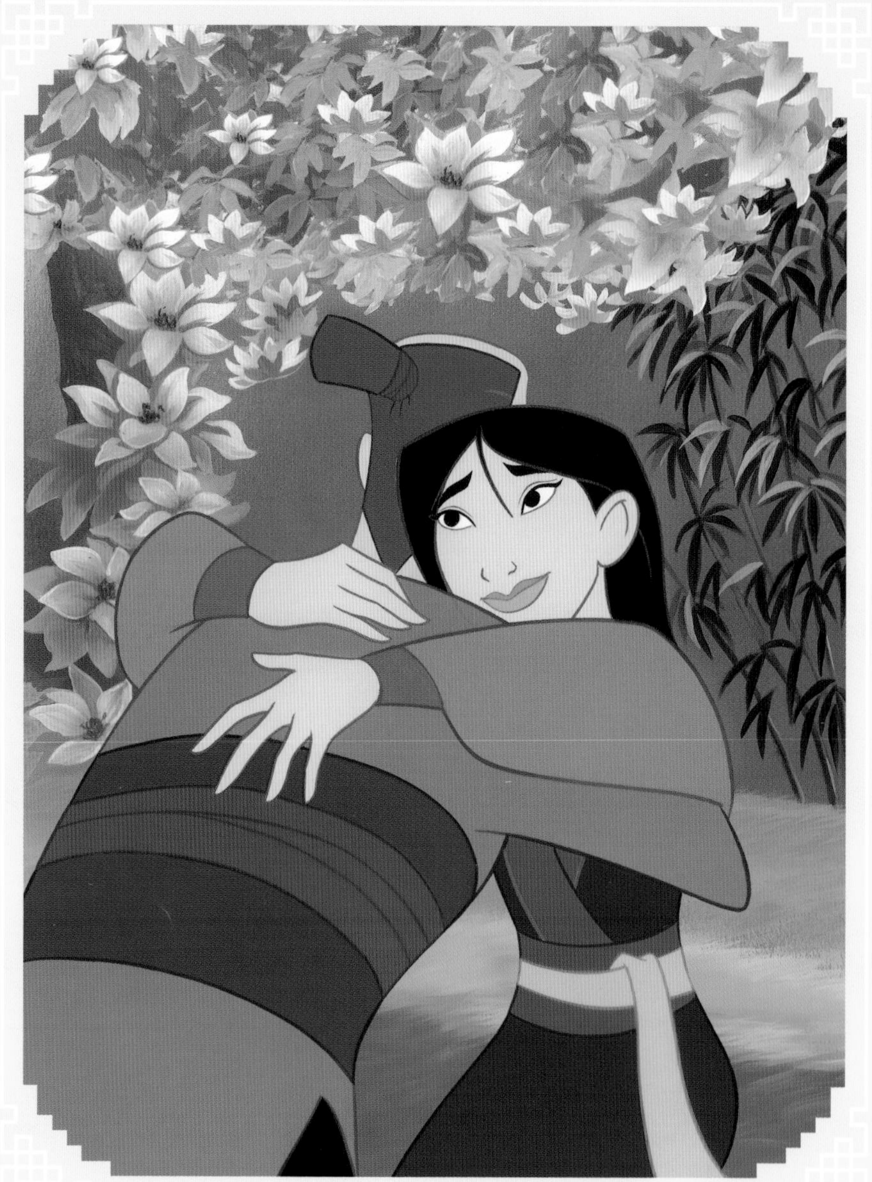

MANUSCRIPT ADAPTATION
Gregory Ehrbar, Bob Foster

CHARACTERS AND BACKGROUNDS RECOLORING
Angela Capolupo - MAAW Illustration Art Team

ORIGINAL CHARACTER ART
Mario Cortés

GRAPHIC DESIGN
PEPE nymi

TEXT EDITORIAL PAGES
Andrea Ferrari

LETTERING AND PRE-PRESS
Lito Milano srl

COVER DESIGN
Andrea - drBestia - Cavallini

DARK HORSE BOOKS
PRESIDENT AND PUBLISHER **Mike Richardson**
COLLECTION EDITOR **Freddye Miller**   COLLECTION ASSISTANT EDITOR **Judy Khuu**
DESIGNER **Jen Edwards**   DIGITAL ART TECHNICIAN **Allyson Haller**

NEIL HANKERSON Executive Vice President • TOM WEDDLE Chief Financial Officer • RANDY STRADLEY Vice President of Publishing • NICK McWHORTER Chief Business Development Officer • DALE LaFOUNTAIN Chief Information Officer • MATT PARKINSON Vice President of Marketing • VANESSA TODD-HOLMES Vice President of Production and Scheduling • MARK BERNARDI Vice President of Book Trade and Digital Sales • KEN LIZZI General Counsel • DAVE MARSHALL Editor in Chief • DAVEY ESTRADA Editorial Director • CHRIS WARNER Senior Books Editor • CARY GRAZZINI Director of Specialty Projects • LIA RIBACCHI Art Director • MATT DRYER Director of Digital Art and Prepress • MICHAEL GOMBOS Senior Director of Licensed Publications • KARI YADRO Director of Custom Programs • KARI TORSON Director of International Licensing • SEAN BRICE Director of Trade Sales

DISNEY PUBLISHING WORLDWIDE GLOBAL MAGAZINES, COMICS AND PARTWORKS

PUBLISHER Lynn Waggoner • EDITORIAL TEAM Bianca Coletti (Director, Magazines), Guido Frazzini (Director, Comics), Carlotta Quattrocolo (Executive Editor), Stefano Ambrosio (Executive Editor, New IP), Camilla Vedove (Senior Manager, Editorial Development), Behnoosh Khalili (Senior Editor), Julie Dorris (Senior Editor), Mina Riazi (Assistant Editor), Gabriela Capasso (Assistant Editor) • DESIGN Enrico Soave (Senior Designer) • ART Ken Shue (VP, Global Art), Manny Mederos (Senior Illustration Manager, Comics and Magazines), Roberto Santillo (Creative Director), Marco Ghiglione (Creative Manager), Stefano Attardi (Illustration Manager) • PORTFOLIO MANAGEMENT Olivia Ciancarelli (Director) • BUSINESS & MARKETING Mariantonietta Galla (Senior Manager, Franchise), Virpi Korhonen (Editorial Manager)

Published by Dark Horse Books
A division of Dark Horse Comics LLC
10956 SE Main Street | Milwaukie, OR 97222

DarkHorse.com

To find a comics shop in your area, visit comicshoplocator.com

First Dark Horse Books edition: June 2020
Ebook ISBN 978-1-50671-749-4
ISBN 978-1-50671-740-1

1 3 5 7 9 10 8 6 4 2
Printed in China

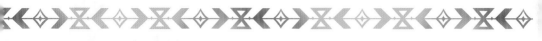

Looking for Disney *Frozen*?

$10.99 each!

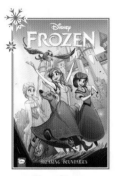

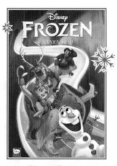

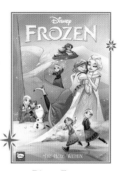

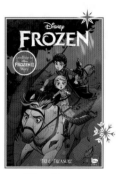

Disney
FROZEN
BREAKING BOUNDARIES

Disney Frozen: Breaking Boundaries
978-1-50671-051-8

Anna, Elsa, and friends have a quest to fulfill, mysteries to solve, and peace to restore!

Disney
FROZEN
REUNION ROAD

Disney Frozen: Reunion Road
978-1-50671-270-3

Elsa and Anna gather friends and family for an unforgettable trip to a harvest festival in the neighboring kingdom of Snoob!

Disney
FROZEN
THE HERO WITHIN

Disney Frozen: The Hero Within
978-1-50671-269-7

Anna, Elsa, Kristoff, Sven, Olaf, and new friend Hedda, deal with bullies and the harsh environment of the Forbidden Land!

Disney
FROZEN
TRUE TREASURE

Disney Frozen: True Treasure
978-1-50671-705-0

A lead-in story to Disney *Frozen 2*. Elsa and Anna embark on an adventure searching for clues to uncover a lost message from their mother.

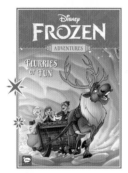

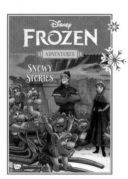

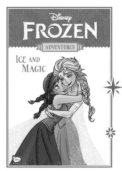

Disney
FROZEN
ADVENTURES
FLURRIES OF FUN

Disney Frozen Adventures: Flurries of Fun
978-1-50671-470-7

Disney
FROZEN
ADVENTURES
SNOWY STORIES

Disney Frozen Adventures: Snowy Stories
978-1-50671-471-4

Disney
FROZEN
ADVENTURES
ICE AND MAGIC

Disney Frozen Adventures: Ice and Magic
978-1-50671-472-1

Collections of short comics stories expanding on the world of Disney *Frozen*!

DARK HORSE BOOKS

AVAILABLE AT YOUR LOCAL COMICS SHOP OR BOOKSTORE!
TO FIND A COMICS SHOP IN YOUR AREA, VISIT COMICSHOPLOCATOR.COM

For more information or to order direct, visit DarkHorse.com

DISNEY COMICS

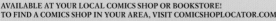